# Queer
# Little
# Nightmares

▼ ▼

# QUEER LITTLE Nightmares

**AN ANTHOLOGY OF MONSTROUS FICTION AND POETRY**

Edited by DAVID LY & DANIEL ZOMPARELLI

ARSENAL PULP PRESS
VANCOUVER

ARSENAL PULP PRESS
Suite 202 – 211 East Georgia St.
Vancouver, BC V6A 1Z6
Canada
*arsenalpulp.com*

The publisher gratefully acknowledges the support of the Canada Council for the Arts and the British Columbia Arts Council for its publishing program, and the Government of Canada and the Government of British Columbia (through the Book Publishing Tax Credit Program) for its publishing activities.

Arsenal Pulp Press acknowledges the xʷməθkʷəy̓əm (Musqueam), Sḵwx̱wú7mesh (Squamish), and səl̓ilwətaɬ (Tsleil-Waututh) Nations, custodians of the traditional, ancestral, and unceded territories where our office is located. We pay respect to their histories, traditions, and continuous living cultures and commit to accountability, respectful relations, and friendship.

Previously published:
"The Creation of Eve" by Victoria Mbabazi in *Flip* (Knife Fork Book, 2022).
"Godzilla, Silhouette Against City" by Ryan Dzelzkalns in *Waxwing* Issue XI, Spring 2017.

Cover and text design by Jazmin Welch
Edited by David Ly and Daniel Zomparelli
Copy-edited by Catharine Chen
Proofread by Ashley Hisson

Printed and bound in Canada

Library and Archives Canada Cataloguing in Publication:
Title: Queer little nightmares : an anthology of monstrous fiction and poetry /
   edited by David Ly & Daniel Zomparelli.
Names: Ly, David, editor. | Zomparelli, Daniel, 1985– editor.
Identifiers: Canadiana (print) 20220230315 | Canadiana (ebook) 20220230528 |
   ISBN 9781551529011 (softcover) | ISBN 9781551529028 (HTML)
Subjects: LCSH: Sexual minorities—Literary collections. | LCSH: Monsters—
   Literary collections. | LCSH: Sexual minorities' writings, Canadian—21st century. |
   CSH: Canadian literature (English)—21st century
Classification: LCC PS8235.G38 Q44 2022 | DDC C810.8/0920660971—dc23

# TABLE OF CONTENTS

7    INTRODUCTION

11   Jessica Cho ► DECLASSIFIED

12   Amber Dawn ► WOOLY BULLY

29   Matthew Stepanic ► GHOST'D

30   Anuja Varghese ► THE VETALA'S SONG

36   Victoria Mbabazi ► THE CREATION OF EVE

38   David Demchuk ► NATURE'S MISTAKE

51   Kai Cheng Thom ► ON THE ORIGIN OF TRANS FEMMES

52   Emrys Donaldson ► INSERT COIN

57   Victoria Mbabazi ► YOU'RE NO LONGER INVITED

59   jaye simpson ► #WWMD?

77   Tin Lorica ► TWIN SOUL (KALADUA)

79   Levi Cain ► GRUESOME MY LOVE

85   Ryan Dzelzkalns ► GODZILLA, SILHOUETTE AGAINST CITY

87   Kelly Rose Pflug-Back ► THE KYRKØGRIM

89   Andrew Wilmot ► GLAMOUR-US

106  Anton Pooles ► CREATURE NOT OF THIS LAGOON

108  David Ly ► POEM MADE FROM PENNYWISE

109  Hiromi Goto ► AND THE MOON SPUN ROUND LIKE A TOP

137  Justin Ducharme ► 75

138  Steven Cordova ► AN INVISIBLE MAN IS HUMPING A VAMPIRE

139  Ben Rawluk ► THE MINOTAUR AND THESEUS (AND OTHER BULLSHIT)

146  Avra Margariti ► CRYPTID CRUISING

147  Saskia Nislow ► INVERT

148  Eddy Boudel Tan ► STRANGE CASE

163    beni xiao ► NAGA MARK RUFFALO DREAM

165    Matthew J. Trafford ► IN OUR OWN IMAGE

173    Kayla Czaga ► DAD MOVIE

177    Cicely Belle Blain ► GHOSTS OF PRIDE PAST

187    Kai Cheng Thom ► FLORAL ARRANGEMENT I.

188    David Ly ► THE CALL

200    Jane Shi ► HIDEOUS CREATURES

202    Daniel Zomparelli ► LIKE ME

206    CONTRIBUTOR BIOGRAPHIES

214    EDITOR BIOGRAPHIES

# INTRODUCTION

**MONSTERS THAT CONJURE FEAR AND FASCINATION** in me will always be my heroes. Vengeful spirits have every right to be pissed off. Vampires know how to have fun. And Godzilla is the monster we deserve. I've always rooted for monsters, and the experience of curating poems for *Queer Little Nightmares* has shown me that I am not alone in this—how loud we are when proclaiming our love for everything monster!

I'm excited to acquaint you with these writers and their works. Each poem subverts the horror gaze so well that you can feel the monsters breathing off the page, as full of life as if electricity were freshly surging through the words so delicately stitched together—like "The Creation of Eve," in which Victoria Mbabazi claims ownership to innate monstrous powers, or Jessica Cho's "Declassified," in which the narrator self-interrogates what it's like to exist "on the cusp of truth / and imaginary."

This liminal space between truth and the imaginary is where *Queer Little Nightmares*'s poems play. They push back on the idea of monsters as fearsome and give tender and truthful glimpses into human desires and dreams. These poems beautifully dissect the heart of what it means for queer people to be (and to love) a monster, like in Saskia Nislow's "Invert" or Kai Cheng Thom's powerful pieces, which reflect on how queer origins are perceived as monstrous, but are full of perseverance. From Anton Pooles's achingly desire-filled "Creature Not of This Lagoon" to Justin Ducharme's "75," which states, "if you don't / breathe in, a person can be anything for ten minutes," all of these poems show how nuanced contemporary queer monsters can be.

I could go on for pages about how amazing each of these poems and stories is. Most important of all is how they explore the experience of coming into queerness, finding belonging when the world wants only to see us as monstrously other. I'm so proud of all these writers who bravely put the spotlight on their own monsters, and I hope that readers will find unexpected bits of themselves in these words. Thank you for picking up these queer little nightmares and peering in where others might look away.

—David Ly

WHEN I WAS YOUNG, I spent a lot of time watching horror movies with my sisters. We watched every single horror VHS tape we could find at the local video store that let underage kids rent movies. I remember one of those nights, during the credits at the end of *A Nightmare on Elm Street*, my sister told me and my cousin Nadia, the same age as me, that Freddy Krueger was going on a tour, and he planned on visiting North Burnaby, BC, the suburb we lived in. We screamed, "No way, you're lying!" but she insisted that he was coming, and specifically coming for us. What should have turned me away from Freddy instead became the landmark moment that lured me toward him. While he terrified me as a child, he became my favourite queer icon as I aged up and came out. He's funny, loves a striped sweater, and sharpens his nails to perfection. Freddy is camp, and he loves to terrorize the popular kids in school. How could I not love him?

Years later, scrolling through Twitter, I watched as users paired up Pennywise the Clown with the Babadook, calling them a queer power couple and turning the Babadook into a drag queen. While I still think the proper pairing is Pennywise and Freddy, it revealed to me how much the queer community loves a monster.

Throughout history, monsters have tended to represent the big, scary "other." The thing we do not understand, so we deem it monstrous. Scholars and people a million times smarter than me have analyzed this through the years, so instead of ruminating on this topic, we thought it would be more fun to find out what the new monsters will be. What beasts lie ahead in the hands of queer creators?

For the fiction in this anthology, we collected a variety of styles and voices, from a werewolf lesbian love story by Amber Dawn to the tale of a modern Minotaur by Ben Rawluk. In Eddy Boudel Tan's story "Strange Case" we see an adaptation of *Strange Case of Dr. Jekyll and Mr. Hyde* that reveals the way racism can create monsters within the community, ones that unearth the darker sides of ourselves. Similarly, jay simpson's "#wwMD?," in which a modern-day Medusa is born at a queer party, reminds us how sometimes there is no choice but to become a monster. These stories ask the question *What is a monster?* and complicate the definition of "monster" along the way. It was a joy reading these stories, and I hope you enjoy them as much as we have.

—Daniel Zomparelli

# DECLASSIFIED

Jessica Cho

I climb into my beat-up truck, bed weighed with one part
whisky, two parts dreams and dirty jeans, then head to Texas

to swap chupacabra stories with a woman who pours sweat
and stale beer. No doubt she's a believer, this one.

No coyote stories will soothe her quill-backed soul;
science can only surrender and let the storm of her conviction

rush down its throat. My gaze lingers on the curve of her mouth
as she says *monster*. I imagine latching on with lips and teeth,

with no intention of ever letting go. That night, I trace
my own body, itself an organism on the cusp of truth

and imaginary, a shadow I want with all my might to believe in.
Under eyes that demand proof of existence, I shed classification

like scarred skin, exclude myself from the taxonomy of either-or,
that in her sight, I may find myself equally desired.

# WOOLY BULLY
## Amber Dawn

**BRENDA HENDRICK IS SITTING ON MY LAP AGAIN.**

The first time, way back last October, passed as an accident. She tripped into my arms during the annual Young Farmers' Haunted Hayride. "Catch me!" she cried, and loud enough that Jonny Pops turned round from the tractor's steering wheel to see what the fuss was about. "You know these fields better than anyone, don't you, Gigi?" The beaded headpiece of her Cleopatra costume jangled against my cheek— she nuzzled that close. "We best brace for more potholes, right?"

The second time was at the Dari Isle. Same as the first, she did it in front of everyone, most especially in front of Floyd. He was treating me to a double butterscotch sundae after the Easter parade. I heard his spoon clink against the frosted-glass ice cream bowl before I realized she was on top of me. "Their chocolate dip is even better this year." She danced her cone under my lips. "Try a bite."

This third advance is different somehow. We're still in plain sight. She could be perched on the bus driver's lap, reciting Dwight Eisenhower's farewell address backwards, wearing only a wet paper bag, and no one would give it a second thought. Brenda's got everything working for her. Her dad owns the Limelight Cinema—the first and only movie house within fifty miles. Brenda glides through each day like Oneida High School is a Paramount Pictures studio set. When she talks in class, the whole school hears her, even three classrooms down. When she laughs, we all laugh, whether we're in on the joke or not. She's a real Debbie Reynolds of the boondocks.

Presently, she's leading our whole busload in a singalong to Sam the Sham and the Pharaohs' "Wooly Bully," which, I'll admit, is a gas because god only knows what we're singing. Five straight weeks on America's Hot 100, and we still can't agree on the darn lyrics.

*"Matty told Caddie / Of a beast she saw / Had two red eyes / And a toothy maw ..."*

*"Had beastly arms / And dirty paws ..."*

*"A whopping size / Matty was in awe ..."*

We blare out fiercely clashing versions until the chorus arrives and we sync. It is only two words, after all. Each time Brenda Hendrick sings, "Wooly bully," she taps her left foot to the four-count beat. And each time she taps her foot, her skirt inches up her thigh. And this infectious rhythmic movement makes my skirt creep up, too. Before the song is through, the back of her bare thigh rests on my knee.

Maybe it's the anticipation of camp, maybe it's the July heat, but I uncross my ankles and let my legs slightly fall open. Brenda sinks into me so that my belly presses against the small of her back as I breathe. I count three thick gulps of wet hay-scented air before she wriggles away.

"Is that the Bernard barn?" Everyone looks in the direction she is pointing.

▼ ▼

"Our communities are changing at a dizzying rate. New developments in agriculture are the way of the future. Farmers who can't keep up will be left behind." Mrs. McEwan skips the Lord's Prayer altogether and launches into what she surely believes to be a rousing speech.

Only half of the Mentors Circle volunteered for Corn Camp—Jonny Pops, Sister Mary Sharon, the widower Bernard, and Mr. and Mrs. McEwan. The Shenandoah brothers were supposed to join as junior mentors this year, but when the bus pulled up to the Shenandoah ranch, only Lynn and Sue came rushing down the driveway. It would have been neat to learn from farmers closer to our own age. Maybe the Shenandoah boys would have let me drive the grain cart for once. Then again, if any of us hopes to sneak out at night, it will be easy with so few eyes on us.

"We know you are tempted by the cities. Yours is a generation of restless dreamers," Mrs. McEwan continues. "Our boys are lured away to enlist in the military. Yet the most noble battle of all, the war on hunger, is fought right here on America's farmland."

Floyd has already muddied the cuffs of his blue jeans, though all the boys have done so far is set up camp. He's sixteen. Too young to enlist, thank the good lord. Floyd can barely chop wood. I'd hate to see him with an AK-47. Mama says an unassuming nature is a fine quality in a man. I'm not so sure.

"You girls may have your sights set on college. A young woman should have her dreams, as long as she puts those dreams to practical use. In farming, there are two very important practicalities: time and money. At the root of both is mathematics. No cookery classes for us this year, ladies! Let's trade our oven mitts for arithmetic. Our Math-on-the-Farm program starts today."

Wasps whirl around Mrs. McEwan's head. I bet she sleeps in Avon perfume and lipstick. Will I grow up to be a woman like that? A sober beauty, a matron of the family farm? I stand picture-perfect with Sue and Lynn and Brenda—four girls compared to eleven boys. Our hands clasped behind our backs, nodding our heads to show the mentors that we're listening.

Except for Brenda Hendrick.

She stares out at the wooded treeline beyond the pasture. As if someone has abruptly shoved her, she lurches a few steps to the left.

Automatically, I reach for her shoulder.        She grabs my hand.
"Hear that, Gigi?"                              Her voice is bright and
expectant, like she's tuned in to a radio station        just as they're
playing her favourite song.

When I make a point to listen,          a sharp

                                                VOID

rushes to meet me.              Hollow          ache clogs

                                                    my head.

My ears pop.
Tongue swells.
Numb shock up both legs.
Stomach chucks.                      The horizon turns sideways.
        A syrupy strand of bile yokes my mouth to the browning grass.
I'm on all fours.   My fingers paw the ground.
                        And Brenda.
                        Always so close    to me.

                BRENDA.

Rubbing my back.                              Holding my hair.

"Breathe through it, Gigi," she tells me. "Breathe."

                ▼ ▼

I wake up to Sister Mary Sharon's abiding smile. She always wears
the same serene expression, whether she's dipping shortbread cookies
in tea or whacking one of her prize cashmere goats between the eyes
with a stick.

    "Jonny Pops said that you may sleep it off. No need to call your
mother," she says.

    Jonny Pops is right. I wouldn't dare risk Mama bringing me home
over a dizzy spell. I've already fallen behind. Asleep in the hayloft on

the first day. Three empty bedrolls surround me. The girls are probably measuring soil fertility or something by now. "What time is it?"

"Quarter past eleven. Rest until lunch, Gianna." Sister Mary Sharon thrusts a bottle of Coca-Cola into my hand. "Drink this and you'll feel better. Remember, a slow start is better than no start." She watches me take a few sips before manoeuvring through the hay drop and down the creaky ladder in her stiff, white-collared dress.

Outside the bay windows, I see the boys' tents pitched in a tidy row along the black dirt in the seam of sweet corn. I suppose that's one advantage of being a girl: we get to sleep in the hayloft, closer to the house and to running hot water. Farther out, three red combines work the fields. And farther still, towering corncribs and steel-sided dryers glint in the high sun.

I joined Young Farmers at age twelve and can be found at every activity they have to offer. I fit show cattle for the fair, raise soil beds, muck stalls, deworm chickens, and pick berries. Jonny Pops's acreage is nothing compared to the Bernard farm, but one day it'll be my responsibility.

Lately, I've been distracted, though. Forgetting chores and putting off Floyd. The mentors certainly noticed something was wrong when I didn't have a single entry ready for this year's canning competition, ending my three-year winning streak for Juiciest Strawberry Jam. Mama says a little distraction is part of growing up. A busier to-do list means a busier brain.

The thing is, my brain isn't busy.

There's this tender emptiness inside me. Like a bruise that doesn't turn purple, still I feel its ache under my skin. And that vacant hiss before I fainted—that hiss has passed between my ears before.

The scrapes on my knees sting as I stand. I pace the length of the loft, kicking up loose alfalfa to sweeten the air. Soon, I'm circling Brenda Hendrick's bedroll. It's obviously hers, with a paperback novel set atop a fancy satin pillowcase. What? She thinks we're vacationing at Saratoga Springs? After a day at camp, she'll be too tired to read a single sentence.

I shouldn't judge. Brenda Hendrick is a townie, that's all. She doesn't need to roll up her sleeves, yet still she turns up at every fund drive. Heck, when she volunteered last summer as the dunk tank princess, she raised more for the community than any of us. Imagine what she'd rake in if she signed up for the kissing booth?

I crouch down and lay my cheek on her satin pillowcase. Smooth. No wonder her complexion is so nice. The paperback she's reading is called *I Am a Woman* by Ann Bannon—a dime-store romance, by the looks of the two silhouettes kissing on the cover. Genesee Drugstore keeps this kind of book at the very back of the store on a lopsided metal carousel that squeaks loudly if anyone touches it. Brenda has marked a page with a gingham ribbon. I check for hay drop to make sure nobody is coming before I begin to read. I only get a paragraph in when it becomes clear that the romantic couple are both women. Women! I reread sentences to be sure, following along with my pointer finger. Words like "soft lassitude" and "shock of passion" and "frantic fingers" flit from the page.

It's filth. The mentors would toss it in the slop bucket.

Is this what's wrong with me?

▼ ▼

Floyd gestures to the empty chair beside him.

"I'd like to, Floyd," I say, "although … I'd better find out what I missed at Math-on-the-Farm." The younger boys hoot as I walk past. I don't mean to make Floyd look foolish, but there's another empty chair waiting for me beside Brenda Hendrick. She's already poured me a glass of iced tea. The sweat on the glass makes me think about how the women in her paperback novel are described as "warm and melting" and "strong and sweet." It must be nearly ninety degrees with the sun at our backs. I drink my iced tea in eager gulps.

Brenda plops a notebook between us. Apart from the scribbled margin calculations, her handwriting is remarkably compact and tidy. "This is the soil with farmyard manure"—she taps the page—"and this is what happens with nitrogen fertilizer. These numbers here show the rates at which sweet corn will reach maturity with manure versus nitrogen fertilizer." She leans in. "Did you know this farm uses three hundred pounds of fertilizer? Seems like overdoing it."

I shush her. The mentors wouldn't be impressed by a townie's opinion. Especially these days, when all any farmer can talk about is how to grow more and more food in less and less time. I wish I lived in one of Jonny Pops's stories about the old country, where a single hog would feed a whole family for a year. I grab Brenda's pen and, in very faint letters, write, *I agree. We don't know what nitrogen will do to the groundwater.*

Brenda flips to a blank page, writes, *Let's see what else we agree on.* She taps the end of her pen against her lips and winks. She writes, *We both like scary movies.* That's an easy guess. Brenda's dad has her working at the Limelight on weekends. She's seen me at at least one late-night screening of *Kill, Baby, Kill.*

She writes, *Neither of us wants to go off to college.* Another easy guess. I've barely crossed the Madison County lines, and I figure I'm never getting out. But Brenda is college material. Why hasn't she applied to Syracuse and Buffalo? Well, it wouldn't be a surprise if she went off to NYU.

I write, *Yellow is our favourite colour.* Her eyes widen. I write, *You got a pair of yellow T-strap Mary Janes for your birthday last year.* Now her eyes are saucers, and I've given myself away. Along with everyone else, I do notice what Brenda Hendrick wears to church on Sundays.

As she writes, *We both like to read,* my throat catches.

Did she leave that paperback out on purpose? What if she figured I'd see it when I was alone in the hayloft? An even more dilemmatic question crosses my mind: What if I hope that she left it out for me?

Could I be feeling *that kind of way* about Brenda Hendrick? And is she feeling the same about me?

I glance nervously over at Floyd, and he's staring back with a crooked grin I haven't seen before. The entire boy's side of the table seems to be gawking.

Brenda writes, *Neither of us can sleep at night.* She writes it again. *Neither of us sleeps.*

"Personal items do not belong on the table!" Sister Mary Sharon startles us. Brenda snaps her notebook shut. "No pens, no papers, no pocketbooks. Where are your manners, girls?"

▼ ▼

CORN upon CORN upon CORN upon CORN upon CORN.

We detassel late into the afternoon. Just the girls, along with Mrs. McEwan and Sister Mary Sharon. It's humdrum work, pulling tassels from the female corn and throwing them on the ground. I tilt my head up to the sky and still see tassels. I squat down to touch the coolness of the earth and still see tassels. Good thing Mrs. McEwan is so tall—the top her orange straw hat gives my eyes something to focus on amid endless green.

Sharp leaves scratch my hands. Debris sneaks into my blouse. I powdered myself with talc earlier, but with the heat wave, corn itch is inevitable. This is Brenda Hendrick's first detasselling, and she's bound to end up with hives. I've been trying to catch up with her or, more likely, fall behind to find her. She's been all but consumed by corn.

This heat is so hot it crackles like static.

This heat is so hot it tastes like stale bread in my mouth.

Still, I heave up song as best as I can.

"*Matty told Caddie / There's one thing to know / If that beast / Is a friend or foe ...*"

She picks up the chorus like I hoped she would. Each time Brenda Hendrick sings, "Wooly bully," her voice seems to drift from a different direction. I pivot left and right, bothered. I barrel through the rows.

I try jumping straight up to see above the stalks. I halt in silence, all ears. And suddenly, without word or warning, we stand eye to eye. I smell sun on her freckled shoulders. A small scab of dirt and blood dots her chin. "Your paperback novel—" is all I say and then we are kissing.

Brenda's lips are sauced wet from hard work. She makes small inquisitive sounds under her breath, as if she's asking for my permission. I nod my head in a little *yes* as our lips persist, and she nods her head in reply. I reach up her sweat-sticky blouse, trace the elastic lace of her bra. Her belly is a bounding pulse. She cups the back of my neck, says, "I've been waiting, Gigi."

*Waiting for what?*

A bereft     VOID     cleaves me     from Brenda's touch. The ruthless sun seems to press closer.

Acres upon acres of sweet corn                                        bend
        to the feral drone that blooms in my head.         Hiss.
                                                                          Hiss.
I barely notice

    Jonny Pops's tractor until he is driving right up beside us.

Everyone is glad for the cold drinking water he's brought. Gladder still because this means detasselling is done for the day. But Jonny Pops's mouth is sour. As much as his expression is troubling, I'm relieved that he's not looking at Brenda and me. I've never seen him stand so close to a woman as he is with Sister Mary Sharon right now. They exchange words in a low mumble. Then I spot the shotgun in the crook of his elbow.

▼ ▼

Our work clothes hang from the rafters to air overnight. Mrs. McEwan left us "farmer wives' tranquillizers": a Thermos of warm milk and a plate of oatmeal cookies to share before bed.

"Aren't we a fab quartet?" says Lynn. "We could start a band." It's true, we were all given the same Butterick baby-doll nightgown pattern in our home ec class. We parade around the loft in our cotton pastels. Brenda and I both in bumblebee yellow.

Tucked into our sleeping bags, we pass the flashlight, telling scary stories. It's the same old yarns at every sleepaway: the Hook-Handed Killer, Bloody Mary, and Baby Blue. Exhausted, our stories are sloppy and nonsensical. None of us can manage to repeat "Baby Blue, Blue Baby" thirteen consecutive times.

"Notice the guns?" says Sue. She swivels the flashlight, bending light and shadow around the barn. "Whatever's been terrorizing the homesteaders out by Agnes Corners is on the move."

"The hippies?" I laugh. But Sue isn't being funny.

"Their whole chicken coop was wiped out. Couple of barn cats, too," she says. The Shenandoah twins live only ten miles out from Agnes Corners. Sue and Lynn make the sign of the cross in unison. "At night there's this noise ... more like a woman shrieking than wolves. We heard it, right, Lynn? I woulda guessed coywolves on account of them being so bold. Until the homesteaders said they saw one run from their coop on her hind legs. Like a human."

"Come on! That's got to be a bad trip," says Brenda. "They're on drugs."

"So what, they dosed our well water with LSD, too? I'm saying we heard it. Why do you think our dad sent us off to camp while our brothers stayed home?"

The twins cross themselves again.

"What do your parents think is gonna happen?" asks Brenda. "Like, wolves don't attack people, do they, Gigi?" She hugs her pillow. I've never seen her look scared before. I've never seen her look anything besides beautiful and unbothered.

"Enough with the scary stories for tonight," I say. "We need our beauty sleep." Sue looks like she has more to say, but I gesture in Brenda's direction, and she switches off the flashlight.

Outside, the crickets have started their song. The barn is pitch black. The long barrel of Jonny Pops's shotgun flashes before me no matter how tightly I squeeze my eyes shut. The last time there was a local wolf cull, I was eight and a half months in Mama's belly. In the weeks before I was born, every pew in our church was packed full on Sundays. People were too scared of the wolves to miss a mass, god help them. Mama told me that in truth, this had been a great comfort to her as a soon-to-be single mother. As the husbands rallied to hunt down the wolves, the wives had rallied around her—knitting her baby blankets and filling her pantry with canning and jams.

Jonny Pops, on the other hand, still brings up the three spring calves he lost sixteen years ago.

My temples ache.    Heartbeat kicks all the way up      to my throat.       Inside my sleeping bag, I grab onto myself,  ·      except now my own skin reminds me of Brenda.

I see her handwriting scrawled in the darkness like a firebrand:

*Neither of us sleeps.*

▼ ▼

Cows graze in the dark. That's how hot this day has been—the cows are only eating in the cool of the night. They pay me no mind as I make my way to the treeline. I don't chance a flashlight, not with the mentors on edge as they are. The stars are enough to guide me through the pasture. The Big Dipper's cup always points north. Queen Cassiopeia sits in the northeastern sky. And Draco is brightest in July.

As I reach the cover of hemlock, lightning bugs take over for the stars. I skip a few steps toward them, arms swinging, wide-eyed. Do we all become children again in the thick of their wondrous light? I remember Mama moving the wooden chairs from the porch all the way to the marsh wood for us watch the lightning bugs' shimmering mating dance.

"This sure is the spot," I say to Brenda as she sidles up to me. Except it's not Brenda. "Floyd! Is that you?"

He flicks a Zippo several times before a steady blue flame illuminates his face. "Seems like we got the same idea."

"I'm ... surprised." I hardly know what else to say.

He pockets the lighter and loops his long arm around me. The smell of butane lingers. "You think I'm all show, no go. Maybe I am, all right. But this summer everything is about to change." It's not butane I smell. Floyd's breath reeks of whisky. Mama says that men who drink their whisky neat live their lives messy. "The guys went looking for Brenda and I said, dammit all, and I came looking for you. And here you are." He scrambles in for a kiss and misses, tongue slopping against my cheek.

"What do you mean 'the guys'? Where's Brenda?"

"There's only one reason a townie girl signs up for Corn Camp. She's farm boy crazy!" Floyd raises the pitch of his voice and moves his hips in a wobbly, suggestive dance as he says *farm boy crazy*. I don't bother asking if the other guys have been drinking too or what they figure is going to happen when they catch up to Brenda. I turn to run back toward the pasture, fixing to find her first. Floyd catches me by the waist and spins me around. My feet momentarily airborne. Until now, I've never considered how big Floyd really is. Gentle giant type. Not so gentle anymore. He bows to kiss me again. His tongue muscles between my lips.

I push back. "What would your mama say if she saw you drunk?" It's the worst threat I can think of, and it doesn't faze him one bit. He claps onto me, not copping a feel of any particular body part, just groping at random. My cotton nightgown bunching in his ample hands. His soused ambush knocks us off our balance. His flailing elbow connects with my nose as we fall.

I am winded as we land on the ground.

The lightning bugs collectively switch off their lights.  And that hiss.
My VOID.



The forest floor fades and returns.
I'm elbow deep in soil before I realize I'm digging.
I don't recognize
my hands.
My teeth    don't fit     my mouth anymore.
Acrid spit.    Skin spasms      everywhere Floyd touched me.
His dismayed face as he waves his Zippo lighter.    Struggling blue flame.
I could swallow that fire,      easily.
I could swallow him.


Not so big      anymore. Swallow   Floyd.          Whole.


Or leave him        for dead       in this hole I'm digging.


A scream surges through the emptiness.

Shriek and call from all directions.        Voices ring and ring until the
horror becomes sweet and familiar.

My own name being called.

The moon is home in the sky again.
The herd is grazing in the fields again.

I see her and she sees me.

She rises onto her hind legs.
Standing wolf.

Her silhouette scorches the night.

                                        Is this what's wrong with me?

I'm not scared. I don't hesitate.

When we run toward each other it feels like        we're making
tracks in the stars.

A gun fires.

Spooked cows hoof past me in a blurry herd.

▼ ▼

We huddle in a grain cart. Stray kernels dig into my back. Brenda
has covered me up with a burlap sack. Early dawn. A thin moon still
looms above. I have endless questions—so many that they mush out
into madness before I ask a single one.
    I listen.
    I'm pretty sure Brenda and I can hear the same acute sounds.
A succession of distressed, high-pitched moos. Calves bawling. The
widower Bernard and his dogs patrolling the pasture—boots and paws

swish through the dewy grass. We hear the struggling rattle of Jonny Pops's old truck turn over in the driveway. Smell the diesel-laced air. Mrs. McEwan's wooden-heeled shoes percussively stomp the length of the porch. In the house, Floyd whimpers. I imagine him curled up on the navy-and-green-plaid sofa in Bernard's front room. I smell blood. Only a shallow whiff of copper, but it makes me panic.

All of it, this saturation of the senses, makes me panic.

The empty hiss that has goaded me for weeks is suddenly full, teeming with every smell and sound for miles. "You can hear ... all of it?" I finally manage to ask. Brenda's question from our first day at camp pings back at me: *Hear that, Gigi?*

She's heard *that* all along.

She's known *what* we are all along. *I've been waiting, Gigi.*

Brenda presses her pointer finger to my lips. She's listening for something specific.

We hear Sister Mary Sharon scale the creaking ladder to check on us girls in the loft. Any minute now she'll find Brenda and I missing from our bedrolls. "We have to swap nightgowns," she tells me.

Under the burlap sack, my yellow nightgown hangs from me, shredded and soiled. "Is this blood?" I say, rubbing the ruined fabric.

"Listen to me. They'll believe that I—a silly townie girl—snuck out and got lost. They'll believe I tripped around the dark and got scraped up something awful," says Brenda. "And they will believe that you—a good farm girl—rescued me from my own helplessness. We have to swap nightgowns for our story to work." Brenda's yellow baby-doll nightgown is as fresh as the day she sewed it in home ec class. Questions brim again, but I can't puzzle them into words.

As I get up, corn kernels drop from my skin, softly clanging against the grain cart's metal floor. Brenda strips, her naked body untroubled as the morning's pink clouds. I have never seen anyone naked outdoors before. Nor indoors, actually. Our school doesn't have showers. After phys ed class, we hurry back into our school clothes, bras and under-wear untouched.

Like her wolf shape, Brenda Hendrick undressed is alluring and strange. The burgeoning daylight seems to arrange itself around her figure. The air grows warmer as she reaches for me.

We only have a short time. Soon a search team will sweep field and forest. They'll find our footprints. Our excuse of accidentally getting lost will be less and less credible the longer we're missing.

Our skins tremor under one another's touch. *Will we fall in love? Can we be together?* But my questions are still too small and common. Our kiss is raw proclamation that ought to be heard a county over, though we're being quieter than a whisper. Together our bodies shake out an unspoken language where the interrogative does not exist. No more *whys* and *what ifs*. The framework of high school and family and county community tumbles under the vastness of us. The known and the unknown, the expected and the unexpected have no relative value in this moment.

In this moment, we remake ourselves.

We are becoming.

And a moment later, Brenda's collarbone blushes through my ripped nightgown. Her bare thighs flash under the tattered yellow cotton. I wrap the burlap sack around her shoulders. She feigns a limp. We blink our girl eyes and march back toward the house.

▼ ▼

Rain paddles the roof of the bus. I lean out the open window and let it soak my face. This flash shower will pass too quickly to quench the soil. Clouds are already breaking on the horizon, letting light beam onto the road ahead. Mama always says not to expect much from summer rain. The more sudden the blast, the sooner it'll pass.

This may be one of the rare times when Mama is wrong. This sudden blast—my sudden blast—is not going to pass.

Brenda maintains her helpless townie girl facade, curled up two seats forward. The Shenandoah twins comfort her. "Don't blame yourself, Brenda. They would have sent us home anyway," says Sue. "Floyd was bunged up far worse than you, and he ought to know better."

Floyd's parents picked him up in person about an hour before the bus arrived. I tried making eye contact as the widower Bernard escorted him from the house to his dad's woody wagon. Floyd kept his head low. Probably more embarrassed than anything. Turns out the whisky was stolen from his dad's locked liquor cabinet. That was the big confession pulled out of him—the stolen whisky. Whatever further account he told the mentors, it did not include me.

Just like Brenda predicted, I am hero for a day, the good farm girl who came to the rescue. Jonny Pops called me his "little tracker" all morning and promised to take me grouse hunting come September. Mrs. McEwan made Brenda and me pancakes and apple sausages for breakfast, while everyone else got overnight oats. Sister Mary Sharon gifted me a few hanks of cashmere wool from her goats. And when the widower Bernard shook my hand, he pressed a SwissChamp pocket knife into my palm—the good kind, the kind a man gives his son at graduation or some special occasion like that.

Maybe I should feel like a fraud. Or worse, an abomination. A wicked thing on the wrong end of a shotgun. But each time my thoughts whir with this hostility, they swivel back to the night sky, to Brenda and me running toward each other, making our tracks across the stars, and I feel unafraid and infinite and new.

So, I accepted the mentors' praise. I proudly tucked their gifts into my duffle bag, along with Brenda's spotless yellow nightgown and her copy of *I Am a Woman* by Ann Bannon. We barely had a moment alone together after we were "found" cutting through the northeast pasture. Quick as a wink, she stuffed the paperback novel into my duffle, and quiet as a whisper, I promised to read it in secret until I catch up to the very page that she's marked with her gingham bookmark. And then, then, we will finish the story together.

# GHOST'D
## Matthew Stepanic

They say that condo is haunted. At 3 a.m. on the dot every night, neighbouring apartments are woken by booms & moans. Men who come & go are never seen twice. When they exit, their eyes are coated with a spectral glaze. They say the man who lived there, his heart is still stored under the floorboards. If you hold your ear to the ceiling of the apartment below, you can hear its soft beat that keeps perfect time, but loses a minute every Valentine's Day. They say if you use your phone as a planchette on a Ouija board, it will glide as if escorted by wisps of breath. If you ask politely, he will trace the shape of his cock on the board. He will spell out *suck my earlobe* or *stroke my taint* & land on *goodbye* before you are certain if the pale desires belong to him, your partner, or your unlocked mind. They say when your skin rises with gooseflesh, it's because a tongue slid over your grave.

# THE VETALA'S SONG

Anuja Varghese

**THE RIVER IS VAST AND FULL OF ASHES**. The rickshaw wallah warns the foreigner not to drink the water. The woman adjusts her sunglasses, even though the sun has not yet risen, and the sky is still draped in purple, layered with the delicate lace of a pre-dawn fog. She peppers the driver with questions—first in English (with poor results), then in halting Hindi—about the river, the temples that line it, and the pyres that billow smoke across its surface. He is short on answers and only points her in the direction of the ghats. He will take her no farther than this. She pays him the agreed-upon sum and climbs down from the bicycle-drawn cart.

I watch, veiled, cursing this half-blind corpse whose body I have borrowed. I see then what I have come here for. Under one arm, the foreigner cradles a silver urn. My kind consumes flesh, not ash, but for the woman in the urn, I will make an exception.

The foreigner begins to make her way down the steps, and I follow. No one looks twice at an old beggar woman with an acid-scarred face. At least here, by the water's edge, the smell of rot that seeps through the cotton sari in which this body was killed is masked by all the other smells mingling around me—dead fish and fire, sewage and smoke.

The foreign woman has come dressed in a black salwar kameez. Black is the colour of mourning in the country she calls home. In this country, we wear white to part with our dead, and soon, the ghats will be crowded with men in white kurtas, women weeping, children scolded into solemnity, all there to feed the river the remains of those they loved.

But what of those who die unloved? What of those whose families cast them out, who will pay no priest to chant over their pyres and see their souls off safely? They are left to the charnel grounds. Not many cities allow such places anymore—abandoned groves of withered fruit trees where dead bodies are left to decompose unburied, unburnt. It is unsanitary, they say now. A risk to public health. But in this city, where once I was young and knew what it was to love defiantly, two charnel grounds still exist: one to the east marked by a bodhi tree, and one to the west marked by a naga tree. Today, you have to be willing to make some unsavoury inquiries to find these unholy sites. Or, like me, you have to live there—but I wouldn't wish such an eternity on anyone, no matter what their crime. Mine was merely to love the woman in the urn.

▼ ▼

In the summer of 1981, Sharmila and I became obsessed with the actress Hema Malini. We bought balcony-level tickets to see her new film and were so enthralled by it, by her, that we immediately bought tickets to see it again. We didn't whoop and holler like the men on the ground level did when she appeared on screen, sultry in a black sequined gown and feather boa. We didn't have to. It was enough for us to be together in the dark, our damp fingers intertwined, drinking in her staggering beauty.

My family lived in a flat around the corner from the theatre, six of us crammed into two rooms with peeling plaster and spotty electricity. That's how there was money to send me to college. There wouldn't be much left over for a decent dowry, but an educated girl was a good investment for any family these days, or so my parents reasoned. Sharmila's people were in Delhi, so she stayed in the dorm. We took turns standing in front of the fan bolted to the built-in desk, one of us holding a hairbrush for a microphone and playing the part of Hema Malini, the other mouthing the words to her song, playing a smitten Amitabh Bachchan in the audience.

"*Mere naseeb mein tu hai ke nahi?*" Sharmila twirling, hair flying around her, singing Hema's lyrics to me like she expected an answer to the question. *Are you there in my destiny or not?* I picked up the refrain, dancing with her on our imaginary stage. "*Tere naseeb mein main hoon ke nahi?*" *Am I there in your destiny or not?* I put my hands on her waist and she put her head on my shoulder. It was easy to fall in love with each other like that.

During the monsoons, my mother worried I would ruin my uniform running home in the rain, so I started sharing Sharmila's narrow bed. Even with the fan whirring all night, the heat in her tiny room left our nightclothes soaked through, and eventually, we stopped wearing them altogether. We sang each other to sleep, except when we didn't. At first, we said things like, "I'm sorry, should I stop?" and "Is this all right?" until we didn't have to say anything at all. I traced my name down her spine, and tasted her on my fingertips, and every day, prayed fervently for storms.

▼ ▼

The figs were the beginning of the end of everything, but I couldn't have known that then. Love had made of me something invincible, and I was not interested in considering its consequences. We walked through Thatheri Bazaar, hand in hand, and if anyone noticed, they might have thought we were sisters. Sharmila bought a half-dozen figs so ripe the sap oozed out onto the bottom of their paper bag.

"My family says I must come home," she told me, splitting a fig down the middle with a painted fingernail.

"You can't go," I said. "What will I do without you?"

"It's only for a few months. I'll come back." She bit into the fig's pink flesh and smiled, swaying her hips to music only we could hear. *Mere naseeb mein tu hai ke nahi?*

Whether it was desperation or desire or both that possessed me in that moment, I cannot say, but in the middle of that crowded bazaar, I turned around and kissed her. I sucked the fruit right off her tongue, and it was the sweetest mouthful I had ever known. The fear and the shame that filled Sharmila's face when I let her go were slow to register. I was still basking in the sheer delight that had come first.

Gossip spreads faster than fire, and soon everyone knew about us. Sharmila was five hundred miles away in Delhi, so I cannot know what penance she was made to pay. I only know what happened to me. The neighbours said I was unclean, my disease a risk to public morality. The landlord threatened to put us out on the street if I stayed. The police came banging on our door. I was charged with an act of indecency. Those who meant to console called me confused, and those who meant to punish called me criminal, and when my father wouldn't pay the fine, they put me in a jail cell for three months. My mother said, "Please keep her there, we cannot take her back." But they threw me out anyway when my sentence was up.

Sharmila never came back to the city, never returned my calls or letters. Sometime later, I heard she got married and moved to Canada with her husband. She always had been the better performer between us. What could I do? I roamed the ghats and alleys, begging, praying, always finding solace in the rain. The men who finally murdered me to make me an example threw my body in the western charnel grounds, and the snakes that held sway there asked me if I would like to stay or go.

*I'll come back,* Sharmila had said, before she smiled, before the fig juice made her lips sweet. *Tere naseeb mein main hoon ke nahi?* "She'll come back," I told the snakes. "I have to wait for her."

"Oh yes," they hissed. "We know all about the waiting. There are so many of you here waiting to be claimed. Stay, then, and join the guardians of these grounds, but know that you will be confined to the shadows. The daylight will reveal your true nature, and you will be hunted."

"This is nothing so new," I said. "I was hunted in the daylight for my true nature in life. Why not in death, too?"

"Unless," the snakes said, coiling around my mutilated corpse, "unless your love finds you and plucks you out of this place." They chortled with fangs bared. "Then, by all means, go to the eastern charnel grounds and be free to taste the sun."

I made the deal and woke transformed. I have wandered the city by night since then, slipping into new bodies at will, snapping the necks of men who realize too late they are not the only predators stalking the riverbank for soft and easy prey. I make madness and mischief and feed on the dead. I mine the dreams of children for moments of joy, and they wake howling at the horror of the monster in their heads. I sleep at daybreak in a grave of my own making, with hundreds of others who live here, too, trapped between hope and waiting, making our desolate home under the naga tree.

I knew Sharmila had come back because I heard our song, an old song now, seeking me out, calling me to follow a rickshaw to the river. The rider was a foreigner with a familiar face and a silver urn tucked under her arm. I felt sorrow to see Sharmila returned to me as ash, but I was not surprised. She must have known before I did that in order to be together, we would both need to become something new.

▼ ▼

The woman in black stands on the ghat's bottom step. She lifts her sunglasses, and her red-rimmed eyes speak of grief restrained. She rolls up her pant legs and crouches, self-conscious, as she carefully opens the urn. In this woman's face, I see an older version of Sharmila, what she might have looked like if we had been allowed to grow old together. I crouch behind her, and she turns.

She is repulsed by me, and with good reason. "I'm sorry, I don't have any money," she says. The sky is turning pink, and I am running out of time. I reach for the urn. "Hey!" she cries. "What are you doing?" I let the veil fall away, and she sees me. She doesn't know what she sees. She only knows she is afraid. "What are you?" she whispers.

The acid they poured down this body's throat while it lived makes it hard to speak, but I croak out the name for what I am, the only name I have now. *Vetala.* We stare at each other, both of our fingers locked around the urn. Hers are warm and clammy. Mine are very cold. I want to tell this woman about her mother, the Sharmila I knew, who threw her head back when she laughed, sang loudly, and loved Hema Malini and me. But all I can say is *please.*

There is a sound from the bottom of the urn, a faraway voice that echoes in its silver cage. The ashes are singing. The woman listens, disbelieving. She is a reasonable woman who does not believe in gods or ghosts. Nothing in the life her mother gave her, in a cold country far away from here, has prepared her for this. "Who are you?" she asks.

*I am nameless. I am monstrous. I am dead. I am found.*

She lets go of the urn. She lets go and lets the tears come freely at last, released to the river, a part of her now a part of it, a part of all things that she knows now are real. I would grieve with her, had I more time or tears left, but the flesh is beginning to come free of this unwanted bride's dead body, and I have somewhere I need to be. She watches me creep away, hiding my face from the light. She leaves the city and what she has seen behind, never to speak of it again.

▼ ▼

In the eastern charnel grounds, the unclaimed sleep, while I sit beneath the bodhi tree, the figs it bears scattered all around me. I tear them open, mingle fruit with ash, and eat and eat and eat. I am disintegrating. I am not alone. My body is a song, and the last thing I know is sweetness on my lips as Sharmila and I watch the sunrise together.

# THE CREATION OF EVE

## Victoria Mbabazi

ask Eve how she became
a monster and she will say Adam
gave her permission

he gave her a body with legs
to the chin a god complex
and a breath of life with no regard
for it he said the worst thing

that could ever happen to me is
a demon with a heart
shaped like mine who looked good
in louboutins and lingerie

he said when I imagine
hell I get turned on I just want
love as her belonging to me
and when she says no
she's a dyke and yes

that means she'll never love him
she says I'm sorry I was
not meant to brave the storm
I was not meant to endure

rough sex and obedient conversation
the manic pixie is no longer girl
enough she says I may ride
the current straight
into Adam's throat

and if he dies when I go
through him
that's not up to me

# NATURE'S MISTAKE
David Demchuk

**I WOKE WITH A START**. Something had been chasing me, was chasing me even now, even though I was awake and seated and belted in, even though the car was still. Ben stared at me, the engine rumbling in tune with his thoughts. "Where are we?" I asked, looking out the window. Endless fields of wheat, rye, and alfalfa swished and waved in the mid-summer sun. "Why did we stop?"

"You were screaming," he said.

"You shouldn't have stopped."

"Do you remember anything?"

*shouting screeching crying laughter twisting whirling darkness clowns crazy arms legs cage laughter scales feathers eyes tongues slicing slashing crying laughter shrieking blood*

"No," I said, shaking my head. Ben gave me a dark look, then checked the mirror as he pulled back into the lane and picked up speed.

"Are you sure you know the way?" he asked. The highway was almost unrecognizable from my last time here. Back then the waves of green and gold were broken up with concession roads, silos, battered fences, and old wooden poles carrying telephone and power lines.

Now the road was lined with low-slung ranch houses, tree-studded yards, and suv-filled driveways. Even so, every bend and curve was imprinted deep in my memory.

"We're doing fine. Just keep going."

"There's nothing on the map," he said.

I turned up the radio. Gentleman Jim Reeves was singing "The Old Rugged Cross."

"Why are they playing this on a Saturday?" Ben asked. I shrugged. Every day was Jesus Day outside the city limits. The song slowly faded and was followed by a folk-pop version of the Lord's Prayer sung by an unusually perky young nun back in the 1970s.

We edged along the river and then out into more open prairie. After a few minutes, I saw the sign for the Tamarack Drive-In fade into view and knew we were getting close. The remnants of a town were creeping up all around us. Two motels bleaching like bones in the sun. On the right, Geary's Appliances and Ted's Garage shared a fenced-in junkyard behind them. Farther down, a clapboard-covered general store stood on an otherwise bare gravel lot, a chipped plastic *closed* sign shoved into the grimy screen door.

*slicing slashing crying laughter shrieking*

I looked down between my legs and saw a pale-green cankerworm writhing on the dense grey fabric of the passenger seat. A sign of spring. I checked to make sure Ben wasn't looking, then picked up the wriggling creature and tucked it into my mouth, savouring the squirming on my tongue before I swallowed it. It wasn't an impulse, exactly—I knew what I would do as soon as I saw it. I couldn't help myself. I had done it more than once over the past few days, in the park I walked through on the way to work, on a patio while I was waiting to give my drink order. I had no idea why. Maybe I didn't want to know why.

"Left at the crossroads," I said, "but go slow." Ben made the turn onto Highway 44, and we immediately saw the spidery steel bridge that cut across the river, linking the east bank to the west. It must have been impressive in its time, but now its concrete supports were crumbling, rebar exposed and rust leaking out in trickles. The silver paint was flaking off into the river like toxic snow. "Now head toward the right. Yeah, there," I added, gesturing past the fishing supply shop to a weathered, hand-painted billboard half-hidden by overgrown water hemp and pigweed, a pasty clown's head peeking out from behind the wood:

*Riverside Park*

*Rides—Concessions—Family Fun*

*Free Parking*

The lot beside the sign was empty. Riverside Park hadn't been a source of "family fun" for years.

"Are you serious," Ben said. It wasn't really even a question.

"We won't stay long," I assured him. "I'm just going to walk around a little, take a few pictures, then we can go back for some milkshakes and chili dogs." He could see I was nervous, but he wanted the nightmares to end just as much as I did. They'd been rare at the beginning, maybe once or twice a year when we first started dating. Now they tore through my sleep, and his, at least four or five times a week.

He let out a long-suffering sigh, but dutifully pulled into the lot right under the creepy clown. We could see now that several clown-headed trash cans dotted the perimeter of the lot, their scuffed red mouths open and ready to swallow our garbage. A faded wooden sign of a clown face with a red arrow pointed out of the lot and down a dirt path that curved out of sight. I had forgotten all about these. I zipped up my green fleece hoodie and stepped out onto the gritty asphalt. Ben grabbed his windbreaker, pushed open his door, and slammed it shut behind him. "This looks ... great," he said. "What's next, we get chased by some guy with a hockey mask and a chainsaw?"

"You can wait here if you like. I won't be too long. You can entertain yourself with hymns and farm reports."

He shook his head. "No, thank you. I know how that movie ends."

"Come on, then." I walked past the clown's-head sign and onto the dirt path leading away from the parking lot. It was early June and warm in the scattered sunshine, but I shivered like a chilly hand had dropped on my shoulder. Ben hurried after me and kept close as we turned past the wind-frazzled bushes, dipped down into a muddy, wet gully, and turned again to emerge into the Riverside Fairground itself. We both stopped and stepped back a bit. I might even have gasped.

"What the hell happened here?" Ben asked.

The whole area had an air of disaster about it, and not just because the rides were derelict and rusting, beaten down by years of weather and in various states of disrepair. Nearest to us were two boarded-up concession stands, the closest painted with dancing burgers and soft drinks, the other with waving bags of peanuts and popcorn. The prices posted on the sides were at least ten years out of date.

On the far left was the Boomerang, a cheap and ugly amusement park ride with small, uncomfortable metal carts that on better days would be catapulted one by one along a large circular track through a pitch-dark tunnel, hurtling out the other side to come to a long, screeching stop where your parents would collect you, screaming and crying. Now it was sealed off, the cars lined up at the ride's exit and the barn-like doors at both ends of the wooden enclosure chained and padlocked.

Next to it was the Spider, one of those tilting, twirling contraptions that was now a creaking heap of scrap metal. Some the pods had been pulled off and stacked along the side. The others remained attached, likely impossible to remove without sawing or grinding the bolts. The ride had looked menacing enough in its heyday; now it looked like a giant claw tearing up out of the ground.

On the right, a rotten, old wooden structure that had once been a roller rink. The rental booth offering boots in all sizes was shuttered. Cartoon cats and mice on skates chased each other around the outside of the booth and around the low wooden walls of the rink itself.

The centrepiece was the Crazy House. It must have been something else at some point, a Ghost House or Horror House; darker colours—blacks and blues and greenish greys and bloody reds—were visible between the cracks of the bright, "crazy" colours that covered the front of the building. Jolly clown faces were cracking and peeling, hinting at ravenous monsters that lurked just beneath. Mischievous monkeys were chipping and crumbling, revealing goggle-eyed rats and white-fanged beasts.

*twisting slicing whirling darkness*

Most funhouses were noisy with laughter and screams and horns and loud blasts of air, but this one was deathly silent. CRAZY, exclaimed the metal sign arching over the entrance and the exit, which sat side by side at the building's centre. The booth at the front was open and empty. An old hand-painted $2 sign in its window yellowed and curled in the midday sun. This … this was where my nightmares began and ended.

But Ben wasn't looking at the Crazy House or at any of the other attractions. He was looking at the cats. Dozens of feral cats and kittens, filthy and scrawny as they stretched in the dirt or darted after each other through puffs of grey dust, wrestling and biting and yowling. All ages, all sizes, ribs and hip bones jutting out beneath their patchy fur. Cat shit everywhere. A cluster of them had gathered near the funhouse exit, lolling in the shade directly below the swinging steel doors. A few glanced over; the rest ignored us. If they had ever known human care, it was long ago forgotten.

"Okay, we've seen it," said Ben. "Can we go home now?"

I held a finger to my lips to shush him, then turned and stepped through the gate to climb the steel steps to the teetering gangway that led to the funhouse door. The first section of the gangway was made of two panels of steel joined by a hinge in the centre. I placed my foot on it, and it let out a sharp squeal as the hinge dropped down a few inches.

"What are you doing?" Ben hissed. "It's locked up! Everything's closed!" I moved my hand along the railing and stepped up onto the next section of the gangway; it, too, made an unholy sound as it tilted down on one side like a see-saw under the weight of my foot. I had forgotten how tricky this was. It was going to wreck my ankles. How had I ever done it as a child? The final section was a series of slick narrow rollers that sped you right up to the door. I pushed myself across them, hopped off with a few inches to spare, and pressed my hand against the metal door with the word BEWARE splashed across it. It swung wide open with an almost cartoonish death-rattle creak, inviting me into the darkness.

I gestured for Ben to come over. He rolled his eyes, but stomped up to the side of the structure to stand just below the railing. "I'm going to go in, take a few photos," I told him quietly. "I'll only be a few minutes. You can wait here if you like or go back to the car. Make some kind of noise if somebody comes."

He looked around the grounds, at the Boomerang, at the roller rink, at the cats, then back up at me. "You have lost your mind," he said. "I'll wait on the steps. Don't take forever, it's fucking freezing out here." And it was true—the wind had taken a turn, as though we'd been flung back into the middle of March.

"You could always come in with me," I teased.

"Yeah, no. That's not happening. The steps will be fine."

I gave a suit-yourself shrug, then pushed the door open and stepped into the darkness. I stood there a moment, waiting for my eyes to adjust. I could see thin cracks of light where the panels of the walls joined, but it was as black as a coal bin everywhere else, and I felt a wave of vertigo wash over me. I pulled out my phone, fumbled for the flashlight, and held it out in front of me. It caught the face of a clown mannequin to my right, smiling grotesquely. I yelped, stumbled back.

"Are you okay?" Ben called to me.

I opened the door a crack. "I'm fine, I'm fine, I just scared myself," I tossed off, and let the door swing shut again. I shone the light all around the wall just inside the door, found a heavy-duty industrial switch box set into the side of the frame. A hopeful push of ancient buttons, and ... the once-jolly multicoloured lights strung along the walls flickered weakly. The power was on, a sign of activity, which was surprising and unsettling. Even if we were alone for the moment, we might not be for long. I shut off the flashlight, turned back to the clown mannequin. Decades old, probably the first thing they'd put in here. I didn't remember it, though. Maybe it had been somewhere else, near the fairground entrance? I almost flicked my finger against its nose, then thought better of it. I took my first photo.

The floors and the walls were tilted at odd angles and covered with crooked warning signs. WATCH OUT, said one, SCENES OF INSANITY, said another. A bloody handprint defaced the wall between them. Another photo. I watched where I was placing my feet until I got to the far end and turned the corner. Something in the floor clicked and shifted, and a blast of foggy air fired as a siren flashed and wailed. I jumped about a foot, my heart thundering in my chest. "It's okay," I whispered, "it's a cheap stupid trick, it's nothing."

*scales feathers eyes tongues*

*blood*

As I moved forward, the fog dissipated, and I saw I was at the end of a long corridor with a series of large, glassed-in displays along one side. From what I remembered, each vignette was fashioned from cheap department store mannequins, chipped and broken, arranged into an array of monsters and maniacs, mutilated victims, and various body parts. Were these what had shambled and shuddered through my nightmares for years? I wished I could remember. I moved toward the first display, vaguely aware of what I would be faced with.

The first mannequin was seated in a metal chair and looked like a naked, screaming man, with a wide black circle painted over his closed mouth and his hands tied behind his back. His throat had been slashed, and his chest and crotch were covered in too-bright blood. The red-stained knife was on the floor near his feet. As I stepped onto the metal floor plate in front of the glass, the light inside the display flashed red, and some kind of mechanism made him thrash around in the chair. As cheap and fake and absurd as he was, there was something horrible about him, something that made me recoil. Another photo.

The second display was unfamiliar, a woman in a nightgown with long brown hair. A newer addition? When I stepped in front of the glass, she whirled and swivelled in the middle of the room, a rocking chair knocked over behind her, trying to shake off the dozen or so large rubber rats hanging onto her arms and legs and face by their teeth. "Blood" streamed from her various wounds and was cleverly spattered against the glass. The effect was more funny than frightening, but something about the colour-changing lights, the tinny amplified screams, and the mannequin's herky-jerky flailing made the scene nauseatingly hard to look at. Photo.

The third was just gross—a bloody toilet with a woman's head spinning and spinning inside the bowl. This one I remembered. Mannequin limbs were hanging on hooks from the ceiling under red and purple pot lights that flashed on and off while a shadowy figure waited behind a sheet hung near the back wall. Had I come in here alone when I was a kid? Had my dad taken me through here? I couldn't remember. If someone had come with me, they'd probably laughed it off as gory and silly, nothing to get all worked up about. Another photo.

The next display was empty, just a flickering safety light shining down on a bare room made of drywall. It had been cleaned out; there were gouges on the floor where things had been dragged away. I thought about it for a moment, then took a photo. *Just in case.* The final window was dark, pitch dark. A two-way mirror? I stood in front of it, waiting for the trick, the shock, but nothing happened. As I turned to leave, I heard a soft creaking sound. I stepped back, leaned in close to the glass … and then, suddenly, a light switched on inside. Just inches from my face was another mannequin, a man, this one in his pyjamas, hanging from the ceiling and swaying ever so slightly on a rope made of bedsheets. His painted plaster eyes were sculpted to look like they were bulging, and he had a twisted rictus painted across his face. Pinned to the front of his shirt was a piece of paper that said, MADE YOU LOOK. Repulsed, I yanked the phone up to take a photo.

"Hey," a voice called out, and the exit door swung open. It was Ben. "It's been a while, I thought I should check in." He looked over at the hanging man. "Jesus. Did parents really bring their kids in here?"

"It was a different time. I think they might have let me come in here alone."

He looked at the room behind me, sizing it up. "Different era, huh. Okay, well … you must be getting hungry. I sure am. Did you get your pictures?" The light snapped off in the hanging man display, leaving us in the dim rainbow glow of the Christmas bulbs. On a timer, probably.

"There's one more thing I need to check out." I pointed to a door around the side of the last display, a door we could now barely see. NATURE'S MISTAKE was painted across it, and underneath, $5—ADULTS ONLY—WATCH YOUR STEP.

Ben grabbed the knob, turned it, pushed and pulled the door. "Locked. Oh well. Maybe next time." He was getting more anxious by the minute. You'd have thought they were *his* nightmares.

I squeezed in along his right, between him and the door, and tugged at the bolt near the top of the frame. It slid back with a squeal, and I turned the knob, pulled the door open a crack, and cocked an eyebrow at him. He narrowed his eyes, squinting into the dark. From inside, a forlorn whistling sound: three notes up, three notes down. "Birds," I said. "Starlings, probably. They make funny sounds." A whiff of stale, sulfurous air punctuated my words. Ben made a face, tried to wave it away. "I'll be fast," I added, swinging the door open, then slamming it shut behind me.

This was it, this was ground zero. A snug, dark box that could hold maybe all of six people. Two bare bulbs dangled from the ceiling, casting a sickly yellow pall over the room. No chairs. In the corner was a cage, heavy steel bars on four sides, solid metal floor and ceiling, and no exit.

Not much of a freak show if you only have one freak.

Once again, I heard the whistle. Three notes up, three notes down. He sounded injured, frightened, but I knew better. I approached the cage and crouched down. I smelled him before I saw him. He peered at me from under his leathery foreleg. He was as skinny as the cats outside. I could see scabby patches on his back, on his long, muscular tail—places where his once-shimmering scales had scraped away. Was he sick? Was he hurt? We stared and stared at each other. Most of his plumage was gone, revealing his more humanoid aspects: his large, curious eyes with their slit pupils; his wide, pink mouth; his sharp, darting tongue; the dewlap sagging beneath his chin.

Everyone had thought he was a man in a suit. I recalled the jeering, the laughter. But the barker had held the light up everywhere, along his spine, around his neck, between his legs, under his heavy balls, his pendulous cock. No zippers in sight. "Nature's mistake," the barker called him. I had been only six at the time, hiding behind a trio of noisy teenagers I'd slipped in alongside, too young to read the sign. I doubted it mattered; kids had probably snuck in all the time. Nobody had noticed me there except for him. I knew he was real from the moment I saw him.

As my eyes adjusted further, I saw a scattering of iridescent feathers on the floor, a tangle of bones, and then the heaps of them along the wall, bones and tiny teeth and scraps of fur. There were worms, maggots, scattered around the floor of the cage. The smell of rot hung in the air. I shuddered all over. I remembered those worms from when I was a child. I had reached out impulsively, picked one up, and stared at it squirming between my fingertips, a round blob tapering to a tail, much like a tadpole. I'd put it in my mouth, gulped it down. I thought about the cankerworm in the car. *What is wrong with me?*

A twitch of movement caught the corner of my eye. An old cat, scrawny and nervous, had snuck in under an edge of the metal wall that had warped and peeled up, providing an entry point. Pulled in by the whistling sound, the cat approached the cage cautiously, oblivious to my presence. The figure in the cage whistled again, three up, three down, that halting, aching tone, and the cat drew closer.

I gasped as the creature's tail shot out and whipped itself around the cat, seizing and crushing it, then pulling it into the cage and up to the creature's face. His razor tongue wormed its way into the cat's bloody mouth. I covered my eyes as I heard the sucking, slurping sounds, then dared to look back to see the creature toss aside the blood-sodden sack of fur. After a moment he coughed up the bones, thick with pink, glistening mucus, and brushed them aside with his foot. Then he turned his gaze back to me.

Three notes up, three notes down. I approached the cage, placed my hands on the bars. "You remember me," I said. He cocked his head, sat up on his haunches, and pulled himself closer. The patches on his belly were moist and runny with pus. He was dying.

"Free … me …" he whispered wetly. Flecks of cat flesh sprayed my face. Free him? I tugged on the bars—they were solid, as were the roof of the cage and the floor. I looked back at him. "Free me," he croaked again, and as he did so, a dime-sized white worm, thick and pale, like the one from my childhood, fell from the corner of his lips. He reached down, lifted it with his scaly toes, his curving claws, and held it up to me. Nodded at me. I tenderly took it from him. A kind of communion. It took only a moment for me to understand what I had to do.

He placed his right forefoot on my left hand, his left on my right. He drew himself up until his face was level with mine. He lowered his jaw—I could see a milky-white tube behind his teeth oozing a thick, snotty substance. As I watched, a fat white grub plopped out of the tube onto the base of his tongue. Then out came another. I pressed my face against the bars, my mouth open wide, and felt a gush of writhing, wriggling larvae course down my throat, my stomach, my insides, then burrow out into my arms, my legs, my extremities. I couldn't think, I couldn't breathe, I swallowed them all. When the torrent subsided, I opened my eyes and saw his lifeless husk on the floor, as if he had shed his last skin. His flesh, his bones, crumpled and dry, like old paper. And then I collapsed.

Of course, when I say *I*, I mean *we*.

When we awoke, we were back in the passenger seat and speeding down the highway back toward the city. The inside of the car smelled like grilled hot dogs. Ben was behind the wheel, his face set in an expression of grim determination. A chili frank from the Tamarack wrapped in foil and a Tasty Creme vanilla milkshake sat on the console between our seats. "Oh, thank god," he said. "Are you okay? What happened in there? How are you feeling?"

"Okay. A bit groggy. It was hot in that little room."

"The heat? Is that why you were on the floor?" He cracked the window open, shooting a jet of cool air into the car. "We should have eaten before going in there. You should have something now, if you can."

We looked down at the food. The smell of it, the thought of it, was sickening. "Thanks, you're probably right. It might have to wait a bit, though."

"You sure you're okay?" His eyes darted toward us, dark with concern. "Maybe we should stop in at the ER, get someone to take a look at you."

"No, no, it's all good, we just need to get home. Sorry to scare you like that. We got some good pictures, though." We turned toward the window and let the gentle rush of lakes and fields and farmhouses lull us back to sleep. No nightmares.

We woke again just as Ben pulled the car into the driveway and turned off the engine. He scooped up the hot dog and milkshake and put them back in their paper bag. We unbuckled our seat belt, stepped out of the car. These legs, these arms, these eyes—so many things were new to us. New ways of moving and seeing. We would have to be careful. We moved slowly toward the front door, let Ben take the lead, observed how he moved, the choices he made. He knew this house. We would have to know this house, too.

Once inside the door, our coat off, our shoes off, we placed our hand on his shoulder, the nape of his neck. "You know," we said. "Maybe we should get a cat or two."

"A cat? I thought you didn't want any pets." He eyed us suspiciously, sensing already that something had changed.

We turned him to face us, pulled him close. "Not pets, not really. We could keep them in cages out in the garage. Two cats for breeding, and one cat for eating." He looked up at us, into our eyes, and as he saw us, as he saw *us*, his eyes grew wide with fear. Before he could say another word, we pressed our open mouth to his, slid our sharp, slithering tongue down into his throat, and let nature take its course.

# ON THE ORIGIN OF TRANS FEMMES

## Kai Cheng Thom

*for Meredith Russo*

we are the daughters
of witches
that they could and did burn
we are the daughters of witches
that they are still burning
& you know
in my dreams, a woman
keeps whispering:
*keep going*
*maybe in the next lifetime*
*we'll make it to the water*

# INSERT COIN
Emrys Donaldson

THE LITTLE CARELESS GODS HEFTED THEIR PLASTIC RIFLES and aimed their orange tips at the bucks. They slipped coins into the slot to shoot together. From inside the game they were gargantuan, each of their eyes the same size as the O in COIN, and the window refracted the smears of pizza grease on their chins into rainbow sheens. As they squeezed the triggers, a robotic voice echoed across the landscape. "Nice shot! Reload!" When a few bucks lay bleeding on the dirt, the little gods slid away toward the Skee-Ball machines, where rows of light bulbs cycled yellow to pink; or to the rows of chrome pinballs, which gleamed under glass; or to the leather steering wheels in the stationary cars; or to the swishes of basketballs through nets. To them, we of *Big Buck Hunter III* were nothing but a temporary distraction.

KEEP PLAYING? INSERT COIN (0/2) crowded the sky above the dead bucks in a funereal benediction. The slain rotted. Each one had an identical brown suede nose, dark fur, and a blank expression. Occasionally, I stumbled over a carcass and watched the pixels at the edges of its body change colour one hex code at a time until they matched the landscape. When one of their own was taken by the little monster gods, the other bucks gathered over the body. They stood on their hind legs and walked counter-clockwise, howling.

The women lounged near the window in camo cut-offs and string bikini tops. When another little god inserted coins, the women winked and nodded; they swayed side to side with their hands on their hips and glazed smiles on their faces. Though they waved to me every time we saw each other, I kept my distance from them, unsure whether they were individually conscious or merely the humanoid fruit of game-brain mycorrhizae. They might rip out my throat with their long, gleaming teeth and leave me to disappear into the landscape, too. Honestly, given my boredom, that fate didn't sound so bad to me.

I missed my friends and my life before *Big Buck Hunter III*. The last thing I remembered was cleaning a dabb lizard habitat at a friend's house, my towel squeaking against the inside of the aquarium as I listened to the television show *Rogue Repo*. On the show, the owner of a window dressing store begged in a Scottish accent to keep her heirloom wainscotting. The lizard skittered over my hand and knocked the heat lamp into his water bowl. When I reached for it, I felt a big buzz and blacked out. I woke up here. The question of whether or not this game was an afterlife troubled me at first. I searched the whole perimeter and found no way out. I tried deleting myself—jumping in front of the bucks, or off the biggest boulder I could find—and each time, a pixel layer stayed between myself and the ground, between myself and some rest. As far as I could tell, I was trapped.

I stared at the ground as I walked, surrounded always by the same landscape, the same people, the same weather. As I climbed a small boulder to avoid a corpse, I noticed a latch underneath a scruff of moss. I stopped and balanced myself between two near-vertical walls as I fiddled with it.

"Trust me. Doesn't work."

One of the women stood behind me, her arms folded. Gooseflesh rose on her bare shoulders. She beckoned, and I followed. Maybe this was the game's way of reaching out to me, or maybe she was a person, too. Either way, I had nothing to lose. We passed through the field, over boulders and through thickets, to a flickering patch of gnarled trees I had not yet worked up the courage to enter. In the thicket was a tent I had never noticed before. Silvery wires winked through the fabric. As we stepped in, she held back the tent flap for me.

Inside, more women with camo jackets and caps layered over their bikinis stalked back and forth and leaned over computers with purpose in their movements. Up close, they differentiated into individuals with distinctive features—a wide nose here, freckles there—rather than multiples of a single body type.

The woman who brought me here took my elbow and led me to a rough table at the side of the room on which sheets of birchbark teetered in piles.

"What is this place?" I asked.

"Far as we can tell, it's real, though of course none of us knows for sure. None of us remembers who or where we were before."

"I meant the tent," I said.

"Oh," she said. "Our hideout."

"Who are you hiding from?"

She shrugged. "Them," she said, making air quotes with her fingers. "Not sure who they are. They punish us if we don't look pretty for the players."

"Punish you?"

"A hook comes down from the ceiling, spears her, and reels her away. We never see her again."

I imagined spurts of blood staining camo cut-offs in a deranged claw-crane crossover game as I searched for something to say.

"I'm sorry," I said.

She shook her head. "Don't be. You're stuck in here, same as us. The others wanted to keep you out of our plans, but I saw something in you. I don't think you're a spy for the game. We've seen those before. They always move the same way and repeat themselves."

"Plans?"

"We built this interface," she said. She moved the table aside to reveal a rock. No, it wasn't a rock—it was a screen built to look like a rock. Light-green text scrolled down over a black background too fast for me to make out individual words.

"Built to look like a rock?" I said. Maybe it was chiselled out of a rock. In the low light and with my bad eyes, I couldn't be sure.

"It's fake," she said. "Got a virus inside." She tapped a French-manicured fingernail on the glass, and the scroll rate of the text increased. "Here's our problem: we need to physically embed this rock into the game. We've tested a few different areas, and we believe the best place is in the glass at the front window. But whenever one of us gets close, there goes the hook, and she's winched away. That's why the rock looks so banged up."

"You want me to try? I can definitely carry that thing. I mean, it seems pretty light," I said. I wanted them to be impressed by my ability to heft heavy objects, by the way I inhabited my new-to-me masculinity. Collectively, the women smiled. I wasn't sure whether they knew how much they made my heart race. They probably did. That was probably why they'd asked me. And I was a sucker for it. Helping gorgeous women through a demonstration of my ability to lift was the pinnacle of gender euphoria.

"What will it do? Let us out?" I said.

"Where would we go, honey?" she said. "No, we want privacy. I mean, sure, maybe we can get out, but none of us is holding out hope for *escape*. We want the game to power down, even for just a moment, even if it means that's it for us. Get some peace and quiet up in here, whatever it takes. We're sick of the performance, of the constant noise, of the claw, of pain. We're ready."

I bent to lift the rock, which was the size of a soccer ball. I loved its grey-green, sparkling heft. For the first time since I'd arrived in the game, I felt useful. I was helping someone. I was helping us all.

I came out of the woods and into the diffuse sunlight. Same weather as always. A patch of grey rolled over the sky and replaced

*KEEP PLAYING? INSERT COIN (0/2)*. I felt watched, so I sped up. I stumbled with the uneven weight. Behind me, I heard a hatch retract and a winch lower. The hook. I did not look back. When I heard it just behind me, close enough to touch, I jumped into a crevice. The hook missed me by inches and sailed up and away.

When I came close to the glass, more pixels prevented me from getting right up to it. I threw the stone as hard as I could. It wedged into the glass, which splintered outward from the hole in a spiderweb pattern. Each glass fragment glowed neon yellow before it went dark.

Around me, the landscape began to disintegrate. The sky fuzzed. A buck pawed at the ground nearby. The huff of his breath moved from three dimensions to two, and his antlers became the outlines of antlers, his muzzle a sketched version of his face. The trees flattened to brown blocks. Behind me, the women howled.

White text in a sans serif font appeared on the dark front screen.

> *ERROR*

> *FATAL ERROR*

> *FATAL RUNTIME ERROR*

On the other side of the glass, the Skee-Ball lights turned yellow, then a white so bright it burned through the dark. The lights burst one by one like fireworks.

# YOU'RE NO LONGER INVITED

**Victoria Mbabazi**

my blood is wine
fermenting I was taught
vampires love me better
rotting I desire

pain that puts me under
how enticing to lose myself
in her I almost forget
my promise to the sun

till she turns to ash in
daylight all loss is temporary
I'm a necromancer each night
I bring her back to life

and with every return
I love her a little less
still I am nothing
without a haunting

I'm afraid if she goes I'll find
her in another demon
love is teeth to the neck
it'll only feel right draining

but if nothing is permanent
hell has to be an awakening
I have to find that loving
half alive will never lead

to happily ever anything
I have to believe I'm deserving
of a love that is endless

# #WWMD?

jaye simpson

*god should have made girls lethal*
*when he made monsters of men.*
—Elisabeth Hewer, *Wishing for Birds*

ERYNE IS SHOUTING A WARNING about something just past the wind-surfers, but before the yachts that always dump sewage into the waters. I squint west and see them bobbing between the waves: merfolk or selkies. Hungry beings capable of therianthropy, pushed out from their depths to hunt closer to shores.

They mostly take children who swim too far out, an established pattern, since children who can't swim as well as adults are easier to drag to the depths and consume quickly. They are more desperate than dangerous, in my opinion. The real danger is the murderous river otters that sometimes make an appearance, like the one that ravaged the Dr. Sun Yat-Sen Classical Chinese Garden a few years back. While everyone was either #TeamOtter or #TeamKoi, my friends and I saw the devastating fanaticism for these hungry spirits running amok. That's Vancouver for you—a city where many can hide in plain sight.

We have rules for them: we don't make eye contact and we pretend not to see them, but stay wary. A finned tail breaches the water, and I see the full threat: a small pod of merfolk, enough of them to cause some serious damage. Selkies, on the other hand, always get caught or interrupted.

I sometimes feel like I am one of these beings, close enough to look human, enough to be fuckable at least, but not enough to be granted humanity. Humans always want to fuck monsters, that's like the whole point of *The Shape of Water*, when you break it down. Good for Sally Hawkins's character, though. Even though she may or may not have died in the end. Del Toro likes ambiguity. I do, too, although I much prefer not knowing exactly what's in the water.

Makes it easier to jump in.

"Hello."

I'd sensed someone approaching and briefly registered that he was probably walking toward the water to swim. Now he sits down beside me, this curious man with a Facetuned jawline and a well-groomed beard.

"Juvéderm looks good on you," I respond snarkily.

The man, who I can't help but call Mr. Instagram in my head, smiles, and of course he has those Orange County plastic surgery dimples. I want to throw up in my mouth because he doesn't even look real, some uncanny valley bullshit with a deep-brown-to-blond ombre and perfect soap brows. A living, breathing Eurocentric jerk-off. The worst part is I see men like him everywhere—every other boy on Tinder, interspersed between skater boys who think they're too cool and soft-boy pieces of shit who think gaslighting boundaries is quirky (it's fucking not). One wouldn't be wrong in saying I fucking hate men, but whatever. It is what it is.

"Weird way to flirt," he says with a half smile that reveals sparkling white teeth. My face is pulled in an uncomfortable sneer, my sunglasses lifting from my cheeks. The loose curls on his head blow gently in the wind. He is too pretty to be talking to me.

"Mm-hmm, you betcha, Mr. Instagram," I say, tossing my hair over my shoulder. It brushes his face and he doesn't flinch.

"Mr. Instagram? Isn't Insta dead? Like the Zuckster killed it with the whole Metaverse nonsense. TikTok is still going strong—why can't I be Mr. TikTok?" He grins big. He's an exceptional Perrier, and that bothers me.

"No, Mr. Instagram, cuz you're completely off base and irrelevant to me. Go post some thirst trap reels," I retort with an ear-to-ear smile. He leans closer to me to smile back, and my skin crawls, the hair on the nape of my neck lifting.

His hand lifts to touch a strand of my deep-brown hair, twirling it between his fingers, and he smiles, almost like he's studying me. He doesn't get from my slight pull away that I am uncomfortable. I have to yank my own hair from his grasp.

A single strand pulls free. He holds it gently, then lets it fly toward the water on the breeze. He laughs. The merfolk have begun to circle a struggling windsurfer, and no one is noticing. This could turn grim, and quickly. I look away, back at Mr. Instagram.

"Don't touch me without asking. I'm not sure where you get off, but that sort of shit doesn't fly here. Where'd your lack of charm come from, 2010?" I grimace at him as I stand up and glance toward the blankets my friends are occupying. They are all looking over, and Eryne is calling out, but I can't hear what she's saying over the waves, seagulls, and others at the beach. In the wind, her salt and pepper hair flows like a river from her head, an ancient halo.

"I'm sorry. Truly. You just look like someone I knew a while ago." His face flashes with a sliver of hurt and then it's gone, and he's crinkling his dazzling eyes at me. I feel slightly self-conscious, almost bare before this man. I cover my chest and grab my beach wrap.

"Okay, Gotye, cool that I look like somebody that you used to know, but that doesn't change how uncomfortable I am right now." I head toward my friends. Their gazes are quizzical, and I can tell Eryne is concerned.

Mr. Instagram is standing too now, only a few inches taller than me, but his green eyes feel like scalpels on my frontal lobe. A blooming headache and a wave of nausea ricochet throughout me, my joints weak. I don't notice I am swaying until he's holding me up. I can feel myself pushing his arms off of me and recognize Eryne's voice beside me, speaking comfortingly to me.

Mr. Instagram's grip drops. "She started to falter, maybe sunstroke or something?"

Eryne bares her teeth. "I was watching from the start, and she didn't exactly vibe with you." Her tone is sharp as she steers me toward the blankets.

Mr. Instagram's face is turned about in concern, his brows furrowed, his arms sort of reaching out.

"Whatever," I mutter. Eryne leads me into Jake and Alec's arms. They pull the beach umbrella over me while Eryne rummages in the cooler I bought several years ago just for the coastal summers.

"Better be the blue flavour or I'll literally barf. Or the white one," I mutter.

Jake checks my forehead temperature with his hand. I lift the wrist that my smart watch is on and wave it at him—it illuminates and shows him my vital statistics. This is easier than him trying to figure it out; he isn't first-aid trained, and I hate being prodded at.

Mr. Instagram has walked over and is standing uncomfortably close. He shifts from one foot to the other, and Eryne turns and glares.

"Better fuck off, buddy," she spits, and he recoils. I can't help but smile.

"Sorry," he quietly says to me. "I hope to see you again sometime."

"I hope the fuck not, sir," I mutter. Looking dejected, he promptly leaves as Eryne hands me the appropriate flavour of Gatorade.

"Daphne, you're literally so demanding when you can't fucking regulate your mood," Alec says offhandedly. I lift my head slightly to flash him a sickly smile and, in the sweetest tone I can muster, retort, "I am so sorry I was dealing with a creep and felt sick. I'll just immediately process that in a way that keeps my mood in check and not allow my emotional response to mar your coming to my rescue."

"Alec, that's super hard-core rude," Eryne tosses out. "You saw that weirdo—he was all up in Daphne's space. Honestly, I would've thought you'd know better, especially since Rebecca."

"That's so different—Rebecca actually totally vilified Daphne in that situation. I was only like slightly microaggressional!" Alec says, and I break out laughing at his self-awareness. Rebecca will always be the butt of our jokes, even though that incident was five years ago, at the free TLC concert at the Pacific National Exhibition. She shouldn't have asked me to explain the anxiety attack I'd had after seeing someone known for doxxing trans women in the line for overpriced Hey Y'Alls.

"Ekosi, bitches! We should get going. It's late, and traffic back to East Van is a bitch at this time." Eryne leads. I am sitting up, sand everywhere, and my headache is fading. I reach for my bag, but Alec is already helping me up and handing it to me. I make sure to shower before getting in the carshare.

Once home, we all scarf down the takeout we ordered and tidy up. The boys take out the trash and rinse the cooler and the lawn chairs we brought. In the kitchen, Eryne dances off beat to a Spotify mix made by some cute lesbian crush of hers, a playlist with too much girl in red and not enough Tracy Chapman or Ani DiFranco. I am one year shy of thirty, so I age myself with my distaste for this wishy-washy neo-yearning—didn't Hayley Kiyoko blast our desire for more wide open?

"What an action-packed day. I think I'm gonna shower for real and then hit the hay. Tomorrow is Peachez n Bananaz, and I need to go to Sephora for that new biodegradable glitter." She twirls and dances out of the kitchen, her braid swinging with her and wrapping around her neck for a brief moment. I hear the shower turn on, and the playlist changes to Doja Cat's *Planet Her* on blast.

The back door swings open. Jake and Alec look dishevelled, to say the least. These two towering Métis men near panting.

"Looks like y'all saw a ghost or something." I state the obvious because this could have happened—in fact, it has. Several times.

"Th-there's a goblin thing in the alleyway rooting through the garbage!" Jake stammers.

"You sure it isn't that hairless pug with psoriasis from down the block? Henry, I think his name is." I encountered Henry last year, and by encounter I mean slept with his owner. Several times. Alec shakes his head, and his long black curls shake alongside his chiselled face.

I stand up from the table and walk out to the back porch. Sure enough, a sickly pale, stout humanoid figure is rooting through the garbage, its head bulbous, its black eyes bulging, and its mouth full of sharp glass. I can hear it snuffling urgently. I turn inside and shut the door quickly, locking it.

"Whatever. Don't acknowledge them—they'll ask you a riddle and then kidnap you. They are the colonizing Little People, nothing like the beings this land had before. Pay them no mind, but also don't ignore them; they get upset if you bump into them cuz it means you can see them. Jenny got stuck on the east side of Commercial once for a month because she couldn't answer one of those little diddy riddles they have. Sucked big time because Jenny is like one-sixteenth Little People or something. You both got away scot-free, in my opinion." I lead the boys to the stairs up to their suite. "Try and sleep. It can't get in."

I hope I sound comforting. That thing was ugly as all hell, and honestly, it has been a while since we touched up our ash salt protection against those kinds of creatures. The beings who were here before didn't abide by such supernatural laws; they just did what they wanted, and oftentimes left us alone if we asked politely. I head over to the chaise longue in the front study, a comfortable lobby space in our communal housing.

I wake to the light leaking in through the bay window, filtered by a transparent film, a kaleidoscope pattern that fragments the softest of rainbows on my skin. I am glowing as I shake the sleep from my limbs and rub my eyes. My phone is plugged in on the side table, and a light teal-and-grey blanket lies atop me. Eryne.

The smell of coffee hits me at the same time as the smell from my armpits, a bitter and sour slap across the face startling me awake. Morning noise echoes from the kitchen: cupboards opening and closing, a deep rumbling from one of the twins, and Eryne's laughter.

I stretch. My phone tells me its dilation day. "Bloody fucking hell." Hearing my exclamation, Eryne enters and hands me a small mug containing a smooth latte. She grimaces and snorts. I must be the most putrid and grimy thing she's seen all week, other than the melting raccoon carcass we discovered in the alleyway two days ago. The goblin has probably eaten that by now, though. A blessing in disguise, if you ask me.

"They're already in the washroom. Your calendar is synced with mine." Gifting me a smirk as she walks out.

I down the latte, ignoring the heat splashing the back of my throat. It's delicious, the brief taste I get, and with a hard gulp I am moving. In the bathroom, neatly lined up in a sterile container is my collection of rainbow dilators and a Costco-sized bottle of lubricant with a heavy duty pump. I have to shower first—I can't comfortably do this while feeling like a human garbage bin. I plan it ahead of me: wash off yesterday's makeup, initial shower, dilation, second shower, shave legs, moisturize, and then skin care. This ritual is as close to ceremony as I get now. A pattern of care is a commitment to myself and the maintenance necessary to keep my highly manicured presentation viable once I walk out the front door or post on social media.

The day is swallowed by these rituals. By the time I fix myself in front of the wardrobe, stark naked, it's afternoon. My skin is filled with black tattoos, some more faded than others, but the style of all of them is similar. Stick and pokes, grey-scale, and blackwork cover my limbs: skulls and plants, symbols and weather patterns, teeth and matchsticks. This is a canvas designed over the years by me and the artists I've worked closely with. Some people have asked if I sleep with any of the tattoo artists I work with, as if that must be the reason I have so many. Why does a trans woman have so many tattoos? The same fucking reason anyone else does: a careful balance of design and flash, with a fair share of cover-ups to hide the practice space a college buddy took up years prior.

I stare at my body and think about when the perception of me was a severe desexualization, a removal of my own autonomy and sexual self-actualization. I was this in-between-gender boy-thing and then I was this giant woman, full of valleys and peaks.

Consumed at every moment.

The line for Peachez n Bananaz is long, and folks complain as we glide past them. They do this every time, as if they don't know what a guest list is, some whiny white girl loudly protests. I make sure to give her shoulder a shove as I pass by, because I am always at the point of exhaustion when it comes to white girls, especially the ones who act too entitled.

"Hey, that bitch shoved me!" she shrills and lunges, grabbing my upper arm and yanking me back. Eryne and Mariah turn rapidly, but security descends on us, and I am pushed to the ground, my face hitting the pavement. I don't know who it is, but his hand is holding my head down and his knees are on my back, my breath shuddering as his weight on me increases. I can't even talk, but suddenly he's gone and I hear a shuffle, shouts and yells, and then a thud and gasps. Eryne and Mariah are at my side and turn me over to catch my breath. I can see that the white girl doesn't have a hair out of place; she clearly wasn't detained. My face is sore and my back hurts. I blink my stinging eyes and I see the security guard on the ground, curled in as some tall butch lesbian stands over him. She steps over his crying form and kneels down next to me. We are caught in her grey eyes that flash in the cool night. Her silver hair is short on the sides, but a long braid runs from the top and back. She's wearing denim cut-offs and a cropped T-shirt with an archer on the front. She helps me up, and I turn to the white girl sharply.

"Better take the word 'settler' out of your Insta bio and honestly identify as the colonizer cunt that you are," I hiss with a harsh C on "cunt," but before I can gather enough spit to send this bitch's way, Eryne, Mariah, and The Butch have pulled me toward the medical tent in the lobby of the warehouse. The only immediate damage is displaced glitter and a tiny scrape. The Butch leaves, fading into the crowd just as quickly as she appeared. A party organizer from Peachez n Bananaz is apologizing while Eryne screams in response. I can't hear her or Mariah—I'm dissociating, thinking about what would've happened if I had just stayed home instead of being assaulted by some white girl and some shitty security guard. I shake my head and, with a slight wave, hush the group.

"Drink tickets, fire the security guard, pull the footage for us, and bar that bitch and her little friends from getting in," I coldly state to the organizer without even making eye contact. They are short and pale with highlighter-green hair. I know I wouldn't even acknowledge this person in my everyday life; they'd be the kind of queer to preach on destroying cancel culture but never hold their friends accountable for the white supremacy and transmisogyny they perpeuate in the community.

Mariah fixes my hair, and before we know it, my hand is holding an entire roll of yellow drink tickets. I will distribute these to the other BIPOC queerdos, and they will hail me as some drink goddess, the closest to fame I will get. They won't know that I was assaulted until tomorrow, when someone posts about it on social media.

I'm lazily sipping some dark, stormy-named drink, and all I can think about is the fact that my brainworm is singing "rise and shine" like Kylie Jenner sang to her daughter, Stormi, in that one viral meme years ago.

Fuck, I'm old.

I'm singing it to Eryne and Mariah unabashedly when I see him in the crowd by the bar—Mr. Instagram from the beach. He's in a mesh crop top and short-shorts, leaning into a small, cute girl with blunt bangs.

"Fruity," I say unintentionally and loudly. Eryne turns to match my line of sight.

"Fuck. This is some real Vancouver bullshit." She's shaking her head, and I can tell she wants to pull me away, but I am drunk and already did a bump of coke in the bathroom with some bear in a hot-pink PVC harness and matching jockstrap. I push my way to the bar with my game plan: pretend I don't see him and let him bump into me. At the bar, I begin to fish a ticket out of my bra, and before I can give it to the bartender, Mr. Instagram speaks.

"I'll pay for it." I turn to face him. Glitter is strewn across his face haphazardly, without care. Messy baby queer. Or chaser. I would prefer the former, as the latter is predatory. But men remain dangerous, no matter the space.

"Are you stalking me?" I smile as the bartender hands me my drink. It doesn't matter that my bra is holding forty or so drink tickets—I want him to spend his money. This is a game for me now, and I intend to waste his time. I lift the drink to my face and hold the straw to my mouth as I pull away to a corner of the dance floor. He follows. Hook, line, and sinker. One dance, and maybe I'll graze his neck, then I will move on to someone else and let him see me with whoever. A messy queer game I love to play.

The room is full of undulating bodies, flashes of skin and sweat, salt hanging thick in the air, lights strobing obnoxiously. The room is vibrating with the music, and I can see Mariah in the DJ booth. Her lover is spinning, and bodies are moving. They know how to curate a beat. Mr. Instagram is shaking his hips in sync. He stares intently at me and reaches out. Gravity pulls us together. I glimpse Eryne before she's pulled away by some cute lesbian, probably the one who made her that shitty Spotify playlist. Mr. Instagram's breath is hot in my ear, but I can't hear what he's saying. The music is too loud and my ears only register the throbbing in the room. I pull back enough to point at my ear and shrug. He laughs, but I only see the animation of the movement; I can't hear it. His hand on the small of my back, firm and warm, is frighteningly comforting.

He smells good, nothing overwhelming. Salt, sandalwood, and bergamot with hints of jasmine. I know I smell similar; my go-to is Elie Saab's eau de parfum, a fresh citrus tease with the softest notes of jasmine and cedar. Eryne calls it kohkum perfume, but it's nothing like the small vial of Gucci on my dresser gifted by a boy who told me it was the kind his mother wore. Fucking weirdo with an Oedipus complex, but I'm a sucker for gifts.

He pulls me close, and the room starts spinning. Everything is rough noises and shapes, dizzying confusion. My ears are ringing, overwhelming my balance, and I feel like I am flying, entangled with this man in a sea of bodies very much like and very unlike my own. The ringing dulls, and I can no longer hear the music. He is glowing under the lights, his eyes dazzling.

"My name is Mathew with one T." He smiles, twirls me around as if I were slight. I can hear him now, clear as if we were the only two in this warehouse. He's towering over me, almost a foot taller. His hair floating in our complex dance.

"Hello, Mathew with one T, what's it like not having an original name? I must've dated at least eight men called some variation of it." I can't help but laugh at my own shady remark.

"You're pretty when you're mean. Your eyes get all shiny when you dig in." This feels like a scene from *Beauty and the Beast*, but given his stature, I feel like the Beast, cursed and unholy. He is gorgeous—he must've laminated his brows, even though that style is at least three years old. Sometimes things just fit.

"I know, Mathew with one T. I designed it. Don't ruin this." I'm not fully aware of the expanse this exchange is occupying, but I can see the blurred edges.

The unfocused glare around it.

He isn't human.

He isn't flesh the way I am.

"I don't care enough to not ruin this." He smirks, and this breaks whatever hold he had on me. The edges are sharpening, tiny silvery threads in the air binding us. He's no longer giant and his hair isn't floating.

I let go and step back, crashing into a sea of sweaty bodies. Flashing lights disorientating me, monstrous faces in the crowd, Mathew's shape shimmering before me.

"What are you? I don't want this." I am numb, my skin feels like it's shedding, flaking off like poorly applied gold leaf in one of those stupid TikTok resin videos. I can tell I am swaying too much, the crowd is pushing against me and doesn't swallow me whole like it usually would. I am shaking my head at Mathew, his lips pulled in a tight curl, sparkling white teeth showing. I've seen looks like that before, in cars and on couches, in the very bed I sleep in. He will try to take what he wants, and I broke my own rule: I openly acknowledged this encounter.

I feel like an ax has found its way directly into my sternum, my chest cleaved in two. His eyes are like lasers on my body, slicing me up to be eaten alive, piece by piece.

"I like a girl with some fight, some gall. Well, I like all types of folks," he gloats, that final comment a direct strike on my gender. I should've seen this a mile away. I typically have a great radar for shitty men and for anything that isn't human. He's too perfect, and this is why: he's some hocus-pocus thing that I can't quite pinpoint, but he's bigger and stronger than the things that lurk in the alleyways and close to the shores. His presence isn't all that unfamiliar, a weird lurking sensation on the periphery I've felt for weeks before now, and always this uneasiness. He's been watching me for a while. I didn't play him; instead he Reverse-carded me like in Uno.

*Motherfucker.*

"Are you like some kind of wizard or elf? What do I need to do to stop this? Throw salt? Solve a riddle? Pray?" I scream, my fists clenched. His grin is clear: I am the prey, and he has won the great hunt. In this tumultuous ocean of heaving bodies, no one notices us. Deity. Some higher-plane-of-existence fuckboy come to entangle with those of the mortal coil, to donate genetic material to some demigod destined for death, some Percy Jackson fuckery.

"You want this. Why else play the game?"

"This is a bad fucking trip." I don't think my cattiness or ramped-up charisma can get me out of this. I catch a glimpse of my smart watch— the time is flickering. Game over, because he's altered the time stream, and who knows if it's been only a few hours or years. It doesn't look good either way.

All I can do now is close my eyes and pray, hoping I'm not far away from my guides, or being kept from them. I know I look like I am wincing, but he will not see my eyes, he won't see my resistance. The thrum of bodies and hypnotic lights fades to an empty warehouse, soft light streaming in from the windows by the rafters.

I am alone with him.

Just a girl, quietly praying.

A flutter of huge wings and a terrifying screech fill the warehouse space. I hear her, but still don't open my eyes. I fear this is a trick, but I can feel the wind of Mathew being thrown across the room. Shoved onto the floor, I reach out my arms to soften my fall to the sticky pavement. I open my eyes to see glitter and alcohol mixed with sweat and who knows what else. I see her, a giant owl pinning down Mathew, her wings flapping hard, blowing my hair out of the tight crown braid Eryne did for me in Mariah's apartment. My eyes sting from the blasts of air, and it's enough to keep me down.

Mathew's shape is melting, scales slithering across his arms and legs, his eyes turning a bright yellow. He's transfiguring into a giant fucking snake! What the actual ever-loving fuck is going on? His body wraps around the owl, twisting. Screeches pierce the air. Scales, feathers, and thick gold blood splatter the floor. I've seen blood like this in dreams. Ichor, the blood of gods, from which splendour and sour are birthed. I'm unsure what would happen if I were to touch it, but this is not the time to test what divinity or disaster could be bestowed upon me. This is my chance to escape.

The doors aren't that far, so I steel myself to crawl toward them. The floor is cold, hard concrete that hurts my forearms and knees as I crawl agonizingly slowly toward freedom. I can get out, beg for protection, and pray that whoever these gods are, they don't want to follow up.

It doesn't matter, because the giant serpent that was once Mathew with one T is gurgling, gold blood pouring from his throat. With rapid shudders, he bellows one final time, spraying the air with golden droplets of ichor, and then, in a blast of light, he disappears.

The giant owl ruffles her light feathers and turns in my direction, her soft eyes fixating on me. If this bitch fucking eats me, I swear to god—or gods, or whatever it takes to take this bitch on. I don't care if it's Godzilla or Mothra. Anything to get out.

"He isn't dead," the owl coos in a hauntingly melodic delivery. "I've intercepted what would have been a devastating event inside one of my temples, but outside, he won't stop. My brother has done this too many times."

What the actual fuck.

"Don't," I plead. I still don't want to be eaten.

"I am not going to eat you," the owl says, in a way that doesn't sound all that believable. "This is much worse, I fear. A gift will be bestowed upon your brow. No man shall ever try to take from you again."

"Please"—my voice cracking in half-assed prayer to this bitch of a giant owl—"you don't have to do whatever that is, you can let me go."

Whatever she means to do is going to fucking hurt and change my life into something monstrous. I just know it. The smell of monstrosity is thick in the air, a pungent cloud between us. I'm already monster enough in my community, the embittered trans woman who hefts around her Indigeneity in order to devastate the white queers from their high pedestals. A monster carved from necessity, or at least conditioned to fulfil other people's unholy crusades in community. I am familiar with being a weapon. I know the wildfire that has spilled from my throat and my fingertips.

"No other choice, child." The owl rejects my feeble fight, and with a shudder, she shapeshifts into The Butch from earlier. Now this is a fairly obvious plot twist I should've seen coming. She helped me once, and apparently again just a moment ago, but now she's cursing me. I can taste the sour bacteria in my mouth, uncomfortable and abundant.

"Why?" I don't notice my own tears until she's gently wiping them from my face, her hands soft and warm. The only way out of this is my own end, to be part of some other hero's creation story. Girls like me never get to be the hero; we are either the maiden in distress or the villain. What is this supposed "gift" she is so graciously giving me?

She must be reading my mind.

"This legacy is one he keeps ensuring. You will be of snake and stone. Your gaze now deadly to all mortal men, any who would wish to harm you."

Rage takes over, cortisol rushing through my shaking frame, dehydration hitting me hard. "Did the snakes and stone protect her? When she was taken on the cold floor of *your* temple? You looked down on her in disgust—instead of going after the real monster, you turned a girl into one! She was never the terrifying one to begin with!"

I know enough of the myths; most of us watched that hodgepodge of a film, *Clash of the Titans* from 2010. I'm of the generation who grew up reading Rick Riordan's young adult books, watching Disney's *Hercules*, shielding my queer youth with books and films on whatever subject I hyperfocused on.

"Fuck this bullshit! You know it's classic victim blaming. You could've just stopped him and given protection instead of a curse."

She scoffs. "Stone is stone. He will come back; he's done it each time I haven't turned a girl. This is as much his doing now as it is mine." She's helping me up, holding my shoulders tightly as sobs wrack my body. She tucks a strand of my hair behind my ear and kisses my forehead. She's granted herself absolution, put the entirety of the blame on Poseidon. What the fuck is wrong with these idiots? No consent and nothing in place to keep them from enacting such harm on people who can't even defend themselves.

"This is a gift as much as it is a curse. No one can harm you like he tried to ever again." Her grey eyes are soft against her deep skin. She's beautiful and careless. She stares at me with this sad kind of distaste before disappearing in a light show just like Poseidon did. I can feel it, the curse surging throughout my body, like a hard liquor downed too quickly. This is the cruel consequence of being desired: never again to experience love because some deity doesn't respect consent. The hair on my body is raised in fury. That shitty man is taking away my autonomy anyway. I look around the empty warehouse, the bar tidy and the room cold as the sun continues to rise. I stride to the bar and in a rush, drain three bottles of water sitting on the back counter. They're emptied in moments, but my throat is still dry.

He will learn to regret this. I push hard against the door, and an obnoxious alarm starts blaring, ironic since Athena must own this extremely dissonant club. I underestimate my strength: the door blows off its hinges, flying into the empty parking lot and shattering loudly. With my eyes clenched in the blinding morning sun, I make quick work of returning my hair to a messy crown braid. Medusa took over that temple she was taken and cursed in; she was worshipped before the Church vilified her. Her face adorned houses, stores, and temples in ancient Greece. This crown of would-be murderous hair will be my first resistance against them. They aren't my gods. With this, I turn around, back to the warehouse, and wrench off the other door, sending it flying into the adjacent lot. This will be my temple now, and I will send it crumbling to the Underground before the sun falls in the west, swallowed by the Pacific. My fists fly, smashing concrete effortlessly, my feet skimming the floor as if I were dancing through this wretched place.

*Mine.*

*Mine always now.*

A scream rips out of my throat and the building shakes, windows shattering and wood splintering, cracks spiderwebbing across the concrete floor.

*Mine.*

I can feel my blood pulsing through me, burning so hot my skin itches. I am flying at this point, my body in the air, bouncing from wall to wall, tearing out the alarms and scratching the walls with my nails, human in design but monstrous in ability. Chunks of concrete and wood crash onto the floor. I miscalculate my own strength again and slam through the wall, careering hard into the parking lot outside, a me-sized hole in the upper facade of the exterior. Impressive.

I hear barking before I see the dog and its attached human. Sprawled in a crater of my own making, I look up to make the briefest eye contact with this person. Before I can form even a word, his eyes glow white and his skin cracks as it turns grey. Stone. His body's movement with his last nerve responses interrupts the stone, cracking and breaking off an arm, buckling his stone waist over flesh legs. He doesn't even get to form any dying noises as his crumbled body descends on me, dragging his small dog by a tightly clasped stone hand. The dog is howling, a disgruntled black French bulldog, biting at the stone arm now, trying to claw its way up. The stone human is heavy on me, but I am careful in removing the remains, reaching for the arm trapping the dog.

"Shh, it's all right. I won't hurt you," I comfort it as I crumble the hand to pebbles and latch my fingers on the green leash. The dog is cowering, yelping as I come near it. It has lost its human, the man who must've loved this poor beastie. I check my cracked smart watch: 7:32 a.m. I free the dog, its eyes wide and full of terror, howling away still. The collar says *Beatrice*. Something about knowing her name makes my having murdered her human even more frightening. But part of me is also thrilled by it. I lift Beatrice out of the crater and she runs off, whimpering into the cool of the Strathcona neighbourhood. The man's wallet, sunglasses, and phone are in his dropped bag. The lock screen on his phone is a photo of him, some girl, and Beatrice. I crush the phone with the slightest grasp, toss it upward, watch as it whistles past the treeline—my strength is astronomical. I hope the girlie on the lock screen is okay. There isn't a thing I can do, other than crush what remains of his stone body under my feet.

I turn to the warehouse. It's half in ruin, but I see the potential. *No more rent, at least, not anymore*, I think.

I collapse on one of the remaining vintage couches and gingerly put on the dead man's sunglasses. Then I hear my phone ringing in the rubble, a ring tone edit of Charli XCX's "Vroom Vroom" blasting repeatedly: Eryne.

"For fuck's sake," I growl, letting the phone ring.

# TWIN SOUL (KALADUA)
## Tin Lorica

every night i brace myself
for signs of human trespass in my home.
the fifth step on the stairs is a dead giveaway,
only creaking under the weight of a whole person.

i wait until early dawn
when it is safe to sleep again.

but sometimes i lie awake

and there is maria, with the long black hair,
eerily crooning *atin cû pung singsing*,
wandering around my hastings-sunrise street.

but how did she get here?

did she come from the richmond ikea,
witness titas screech and kiss at each other?
long for a home, a ring,
o *masanting a baba'i?*

my cold hands interrogate the noise,
carefully feeling the vibrations
of each verse's syllables over the floorboards.

the unease of sunday mass
and basement catechism

how we no longer sing our own songs.

her voice oscillates in and out
as she passes homes with heritage plaques—
none of which she can enter.

her body a noiseless, legless silhouette,
only her barren hymn making its way
directly under my window

as if to prophesize once again
that the spanish are coming,
the americans are coming,
the japanese are coming,

and that there are no poets laureate
among the riverbank people.

# GRUESOME MY LOVE

Levi Cain

**MY GIRLFRIEND HAS A BELLY LIKE AN UNFILLED BOWL** and teeth that I
don't get to file until we reach our six-month anniversary. She looks at
least thirty feet tall in our bedroom and has a raw-looking mouth that
seems constantly in motion. She's hungry for anything I can give her,
but she prefers secrets even to scapulae. I feed her all my tragedies as
appetizers: the first time I skinned my knee when I was still learning
how to ride a bicycle, the smell of the lilacs on my grandfather's grave,
how I broke my nose twice and it never healed properly. My girlfriend
puts her head on my knee and croons something without words. When
I ask her to translate, she laughs. "I'll teach you someday," she prom-
ises, and flicks her forked tongue at me when I roll my eyes.

Although we've been dating for years, she still has not met my parents. We sent a holiday card with both of us posing in our living room,
my head resting against the beautiful cavern of her chest, but it was
immediately returned. "Guess they moved," I tell her regretfully, and
she sighs, the windows shuddering with the noise. I want to soothe
her, but I remember the drone of my parents' sobs when I first told

them about my new girlfriend. They had whimpered for so long about blasphemy and damnation that I had to disconnect the call.

"You think they'd wanna meet their only child's new lover," my girlfriend sniffs, and she sulks until I give her a present from the downstairs neighbours. When we first tried making the rounds in the building, eager to meet our new neighbours, they weren't welcoming. The husband passed out, the wife spat at us. And now look what they've given us: ventricles and arteries glowing like rubies, wrapped in their Christmas tissue paper.

"Oh honey! You shouldn't have!" she gasps, and allows me to tie back her decaying hair with a vein. Below our feet, the neighbours are growing soft and bloated in their armchairs, their foaming mouths as pink as the peonies that I bought her earlier that morning—just because the morning was gorgeous, and so was she. It's impossible to look at her and not want to give her things, whether it's the world or a femur.

In the crevices of the internet, there are whispers about a towering shape of death emerging from the mountain ranges and hurtling toward the cities, desperate to kick-start the end of days. People say that she is an urban legend, a fever dream, the consequence of climate change. Once we're able to move in together, the comments get worse: everyone has something awful to say about her gorgeously wretched hum, which puts me into a sweet sleep after long shifts. They say it drives people to insanity, that there are those who die from the anticipation before they even see her; they say that our home must be cleansed with fire. Someone even reveals our address and phone numbers to the nearest precinct, as if we were doing anything but trying to live good, full lives together.

When the police come with their battering ram, I simply turn on the radio and swing her around, feeling the beam of her foul laugh on my skin. She folds herself in half to rest her rotting head on my shoulder, her eyes wetting the cotton of my shirt. "I'm so happy, baby," she says to me, and keeps a contented smile even as the officers burst through the door, knocking it off its hinges. I turn the radio's volume up while my girlfriend neatly removes their kneecaps from their sockets and asks me if I've done the laundry yet.

"Later tonight, I promise," I tell her.

She rolls her magnificent and terrible eyes. A shrieking officer reaches a quivering hand toward my ankle, and she gingerly brushes him away with her foot, dislodging only two of his knucklebones. "Don't just forget again," she scolds me gently, then heads to the kitchen to grab the mop and bucket. She's tidy, I tell all of our accusers, a real neat freak—you wouldn't believe how much cleaning she can get done on a quiet Sunday afternoon.

It's hard to imagine not knowing her. I can't picture not being able to walk down the hallway and see my girlfriend crouching in the bathroom, tapping her hip against the counter as she uses the mayor's phalanges to pick marrow out of her teeth.

Years ago, I had wandered completely by chance into the part of the world where she lived. I heard her joyful song before I saw her approaching my friends' winter cabin, where we were huddled together for warmth against a terrible storm. I was the first to see her ambling up from the heavy white gloom, her eyes burning like hot coals, snowflakes dripping from her eyelashes.

Our first date had been that night. Without trembling, I had let her trace a hooked nail over my heart. "You should be terrified," she reminded me. Back then, she was not yet someone who snored in our narrow bed and forgot to load the dishwasher, but instead, just an obelisk of a woman roaming the forest, carrying my childhood friend's head like a new purse.

"I am," I told her. "I'm terrified you don't like me as much as I like you."

She smiled. One of her teeth had been broken during the scuffle with my friends, and it was as jagged and bright as quartz. When I put my finger to it, she kissed it and did not even try to draw blood.

When we finally returned to the city, nobody wanted anything to do with us. Nobody responded to our brunch invitations or RSVPed to the engagement party, even though it was months after Mitchell and Anwar and everyone else's funerals. My cousins, whom I had grown up with, left in a mass exodus, their landlines as dead as the neighbours. My aunt demanded that I not call her anymore and howled that I was cursed and would learn the truth of myself on Judgment Day. My great-uncle, who was in hospice, disappeared overnight.

The last I heard, he was in Lagos or maybe Queensland. The only one who remains is my granny. "You come over sometime," she croaks over the phone. "Bring that thing with you."

"Now, Granny, honestly," I say reproachfully, but when I tell my girlfriend, she smiles so hard that her face nearly splits in two. She spends a week perfecting a stew that permeates not only the building, but the block; up until the morning we leave, we see people resting face down on the street. We can barely get out of the parking lot—it's a real problem. We almost have a fight, but my girlfriend and I manage to work it out, the way we always do. I ask her not to cook anything that mimics the smell of perdition if she can't *also* make sure that she has time to shovel us out afterward, and she asks me to wake her up earlier to do the shovelling if I've noticed it becoming a nuisance, rather than waiting until we're already fifteen minutes behind schedule. Communication is important, we remind each other, as we clear a path and stuff our building superintendent into the trunk of my tiny Subaru—it's the foundation of a healthy relationship.

The moment we pull into the gravel driveway, Granny rushes out in her house slippers with a candle clutched in her hand. She screams prayers at us until I reverse and speed away. We wouldn't have been able to walk in, anyway; there's heaps of sea salt covering the entrance. My girlfriend doesn't say a word the whole hour-long trip back. She scratches at the welts on her withered forearms and leans her head against the window. I take one hand off the steering wheel and reach out to her, feathering my fingertips against her waxy skin.

"Don't," she bites. Later that night, she crouches by the glow of our tiny television and picks her teeth sourly with a leftover metacarpal. As an apology, I drill holes in my old baby teeth and leave them on her pillow. She wears them on our weekly date night, the teeth glittering like pearls in her earlobes. In the darkness of the abandoned restaurant, they're the only thing that can be seen.

I give her other presents, too: both of the landlord's kidneys steamed on a bed of arugula, just the way I know she likes after a hard day. When my doubles partner complains about his Achilles tendon, I liberate it from him. My girlfriend takes it carefully in her wicked hands and rounds it out until it is a salad spoon.

I'd never tell her, but getting gifts like this isn't always easy. People usually leave for the afterlife quickly, but sometimes they're hard headed and want to stick around out of bitterness or some half-baked attempt at revenge. Those whining spirits settle around my girlfriend's head like curls, or else linger inside the foyer, crowding all of the exits. "Murderer!" they accuse me. "How could you! How could you!" I shrug at them and answer the same way every time: "I'm in love. Isn't that wonderful?" But not everyone can be happy for you, I guess. My granny doesn't contact me at all anymore, not even when my girlfriend sends her thoughtful packages in the mail: swatches of our hair tied together, vertebrae picked clean, a wreath of muscles. They're all sent back immediately, unopened and with a bundle of sage taped to them.

What's worse is that the whole apartment complex seems to be researching ways to make my girlfriend feel unwelcome. She can't take a single step outside the door without being confronted by priests or having holy water thrown on her. She never complains, but I know her feelings are hurt when we are turned away from the complex-wide potluck. "Out, devils!" they chant from inside the foyer, until my girlfriend begins to wail, a sonic boom of hurt that makes their ears grow rosy with blood. After they faint, and the glass shatters, we pick through their bodies and try on their kneecaps as hats. More ghosts start haunting the complex, but we refuse to move. Don't we have the right to a happy home, to be wrapped up in our impossible love?

On the television, the president pats his forehead with a handkerchief and says something must be done about the beast. He will deploy SWAT teams, the CIA, the FBI. The Pope, if he can make it. "Let them come," my girlfriend sneers, and holds me like a threat.

# GODZILLA, SILHOUETTE AGAINST CITY

**Ryan Dzelzkalns**

Oh, Ghidorah
      I can taste your sweaty palms from here.
     Godzilla means *heart-*
       *breaker* in Japanese     but you've never believed me.
    And though you become
       a hopeful tide swelling
               onto my chest
            my lips and though
       we begin the hot-bodied things
   you whistle,
   *can we take this slow?*
              But already
     my atomic heart has blown
       and I laugh, *I've never been hurt before.*


  And before my eyes
 you lose your zephyr—
     the fearsome Ghidorah,
       just a little man
     with bat wings
sorting the lamplight
into pants and socks    a tsunami wall    your face    a sluice gate.


     Down the stairs I hum
     the song of Tokyo burning,
           a tune
          that will slink back to you
         each time you think,

*I never want*
*to be hurt*
*again.*

# THE KYRKØGRIM

Kelly Rose Pflug-Back

Press your lips to the keyhole
on the year's longest night
and renounce all belief,
white face of the chapel
engulfed
by spires
of black pine,

charred bones of ruminants
in its foundation
inhumed
in wombs
of shed black wool

flanked by wreaths
of desiccated flowers,

the severed feet of swans,

fetal horses, white-fleshed
inside pearlescent cauls.

Centuries pass
and I too take on an animal's
form,
chained and pacing,
guard hairs bristling
from my spine—

my vision blurring
in midday traffic

remembering her breath,
heady with spirits
close to my ear.

Below empty pews
furred in lichens,
remains
of a sacrifice

join the loam.

There is no such thing as loss:
only the way we let go of things
the way they let us go.

Forks in the road, like the intersection
where I saw her last
holding me forever
in the halo
of the street light.

Where we spilled
our heathen blood, once-
bitter sting of blow
laced with crystal shard.
Where we fed ourselves
to the land.

# GLAMOUR-US

Andrew Wilmot

**THE HALOGEN LIGHT ABOVE THE BATHROOM MIRROR** strobes like cut frames from a film reel. I like the effect. I angle myself a little to the left, and the flicker casts just enough of a shadow to withhold anything truly identifying: my stomach is outlined such that I look narrow without appearing muscular, and my chest and shoulders, while defined, do not elicit a gendered response one way or another. I wear, visibly and internally, the scars of late–high school anorexia, never fully in the past. It colours my perception, how I see the soft patch of fat just above my waistline—something I wish I could directly target, cleave from my body's context.

I turn to the other side, and the light catches in such a way that with my head and lower half removed, with only my midsection spliced into frame, separate from the rest of me, the hurdles of material reality disappear.

And the blood. It, too, vanishes.

A trick of the light. That's all it is.

▼ ▼

"*Dr. Jekyll and Sister Hyde* is a mess," Daneesha said, quite adamantly. "It's offensive, and I fucking hate it."

"Look," Alicia said, "I know it's not, like, essential queer canon viewing or anything, but—"

Daneesha sighed. "You're about to defend this trash, aren't you?"

"Yes, and it's not trash."

"The movie hates trans people, Alicia. *Hates*."

Alicia kissed her teeth. "Oh, it does *not*."

Daneesha stabbed each point with a finger, careful not to drop their joint: "Jekyll makes his serum from a dead woman, turns into Martine Fucking Beswick, and then, post-transition, starts killing sex workers to harvest their essences or whatever, all to maintain this ... illusion. The movie flat out portrays trans women as delusional, psychotic killers."

"Bullshit," Alicia said, taking the joint from Daneesha. "Sister Hyde isn't some psycho. She's found her true self and wants more than anything to keep it, no matter the cost. It's all metaphor. Next you're going to tell me Wes Craven was actually advocating for some sort of teenage genocide."

Daneesha stared out over the roof's edge, looking quietly pissed. Wasn't the first time Alicia had pushed her into a corner like this. "Point remains," they said at last, "there are better transition narratives."

"Speaking of," I said, "either of you see the news? Eternia's holding an open house this weekend for trans people."

"I can't believe they just lifted that name from *Masters of the Universe* and not one person on staff said 'hold up a minute.'" Alicia shook her head.

"Nothing doin'," Daneesha said. "My fluid ass is never getting a halo. I don't want to live in any skin that ain't already mine."

"But it is yours," Alicia said, exhaling a long plume of smoke. "What do you think a clone is?"

"It's not my brain in there, is it?"

"Well, not identically, but the transfer process—"

Daneesha held up their hand.

"Neesh, if you'd just listen—"

But Daneesha shook their head defiantly. The response wasn't surprising. Synths had been on the market now for the better part of a decade, but trust was still low. For many, the cost was still disgustingly prohibitive. It made sense, though—it was an expensive proposition to capture and upload one's consciousness to a fresh-from-the-petri-dish clone. Even more so if you wanted to make any alterations to your body's factory settings—new upholstery, two doors instead of four, some new chromosomes to fuck with the "but what about gametes!" crowd.

For Alicia, who I'd known since high school, the matter was more steadfastly binary. For her, going synth was a way to bypass the painful middle ground she'd witnessed with so many transitions. "It's all so physically and psychologically draining," she'd said one night a year or so back. "Why put myself through all that if I don't have to?"

"Because it's part of the journey," Daneesha had told her flatly.

Their argument was reflective of a growing schism in the trans community between those still forced to undergo years of psychological assessments and gradual hormone treatment and the "new breed"—those who could afford to go to sleep in one body and slide into another like a piece of perfectly tailored clothing. Ignoring, as most did, that to "go to sleep" meant "dying." Such semantics, however, seemed less important as time went on.

Alicia sighed. "Forget it."

That was the last anyone spoke of the matter. We finished the joint and took the stairs down from the roof to Alicia's condo on the seventh floor, then said our goodbyes. Two weeks later, Alicia got a job with an advertising firm in the city. We haven't seen or heard from her in six months.

"It happens," Daneesha said last night on the phone. "People get jobs, they get new lives and new friends, and that's the end of it. They vanish on you like cash on a Friday night. Speaking of, we still good for tomorrow?"

▾ ▾

I met Daneesha outside the Vancouver Art Gallery's south entrance. She was sitting on the concrete steps, staring languidly at an installation erected on the gallery's lawn: a silver camper of classic look and feel, its rounded edges straight out of the sixties—vivisected like an autopsy. Half plates and half glasses sat half-full on the half table at the centre.

"Life, interrupted?"

They looked to me. "I'm sure there's a wonderfully self-indulgent artist statement to that effect," they said, standing. "Something to do with memorializing the white middle class, or some shit."

"Woe be to the dying breed." I extended my arm. "Shall we?"

*In Memoriam.* The exhibition was a collection of paintings, sculptures, found object constructions, and installations: people holding up bank loans and mortgages; a still life of an RRSP, of a savings account flush with income; brass rings and gold watches placed delicately atop crushed velvet, denoting not just years, but decades spent in the same impossibly stable job.

I found myself looking, as I often did, more at the people wandering through the exhibition than at the art itself, noting several wealthy-looking patrons with clear arrowhead scars on the backs of their necks—tiny ridges of protruding keloid tissue marking a halo's point of entry. The dozen or so people I counted with said scars had made sure they were quite visible, with low collars, open-backed dresses, hair worn up in buns or draped over shoulders. Either they were clones, or they would be someday, and they wanted everyone to know it. Immortality as a fashion statement—the ultimate in you'll-never-fucking-be-able-to-afford-this-ness.

Daneesha paid them little more than passing, dismissive glances. "They glisten," they whispered at me at one point. "Their bodies don't even look real."

In among the synths, an individual caught my eye. A beautiful, tall man with a fade of black hair and a finely drawn jaw. He wore a black leather vest over a white shirt with the sleeves rolled up. Both forearms were heavily tattooed, the black ink receding into his dark-brown skin. As I continued to stare, the man appeared to shimmer in three dimensions, as if his entire body were liquid. The rippling started at his head and worked its way down to his very bright-red-like-they'd-never-been-outside sneakers—which suddenly were a pair of glossy black heels. I looked up again, and in his place now was a statuesque woman with thick, beautiful black hair braided to her lower back.

I squeezed Daneesha's hand. "Did you just see that?"

"What?"

I pointed with my chin. "That woman over there?"

"She's cute. Definitely your type."

"She was a dude."

They glared at me. "So?"

"No, I mean, like, just two seconds ago. He was standing there in a pair of bright-red kicks and a black vest, and then this sort of … shimmer happened, and it was like someone flipped a television channel to a new show."

"Or turned on a filter."

"Yeah! Just like that."

"No, I mean that's exactly—" They sighed and pointed to the woman's wrist, at a narrow silver bracelet with a glowing purple LED orbiting the length of it.

"Wait, for real? A Glamour?"

I recalled the conversation we'd had some time ago, when rumours about them first started flying. The device worked similar to a brain leech—it reads a person's thoughts and adjusts their "self-visualization," as Daneesha had phrased it, making a point of accentuating the scare quotes. "It was this whole thing a few years back," they explained, "like externalized VR for wounded soldiers and burn victims and amputees who can't afford to synth up."

"That's a bit ableist, isn't it?" I'd said.

"If forced, sure, but this is pure luxury. Never gained any traction, though. I heard at some point that psychologists were recommending it for trans patients, to better visualize their goals."

Now, staring at it, witnessing the effect for myself, I was taken aback.

"It's ... kind of incredible, actually."

Daneesha let go of my hand. "It's gross," they said. "I don't like it."

"What's not to like?"

They turned and headed for the exit. I followed them outside, found them staring out at the intersection at Robson and Howe.

"Neesh, I'm sorry if I ... I just don't understand."

They shook their head. "Nothing to understand. I mean, if you can afford it and it works for you, then great. I just don't like it."

"Yeah, I get that. I just don't get why."

They turned. "Because I don't need an article of clothing to feel any more me." They pointed to the crowd inside the gallery. "That sort of thing ... it isn't for me. It isn't for us. It's for *them*. It's no better than a salve. It tells others how to speak or respond to us, how to treat us, instead of just treating us like ..."

"Like what?"

"Like human beings."

▼ ▼

I thought a lot that night about what Daneesha had said. I could understand their frustration. Sort of. But standing in my bathroom the next morning, staring at what I had to work with, I couldn't help but wonder what it would be like to be able to shift effortlessly between identities.

Beyond the cost, which was indeed considerable, the tech was like nothing I'd ever seen. It afforded each user the opportunity to craft a personalized avatar—the image of yourself as you wanted to appear to the world. It was imperfect, though. Three weeks after *In Memoriam*, now knowing what to look for, I caught sight of a man walking down the street at night outside of Pacific Centre. A car turned a corner with its high beams on, and the harsh light reflecting off the glass appeared to tear through him, revealing the feminine form beneath what had been an otherwise masculine shell. The effect lasted only seconds, but it was as if the person had been split across the midsection like a matryoshka doll. They hugged their sides, embarrassed at how exposed they were, while their outer shell reconstituted itself, checkered lights knitting themselves together again.

It was called "strobing." I learned about it on a Reddit forum called "r/GoingGlam"—the filtration system struggled with light refraction and accommodating multiple strong light sources all at once. It didn't seem like anything more than an inconvenience.

My curiosity remained piqued.

▼ ▼

Two weeks later, the Ghost of Queerness Past showed up on my doorstep with a smile and a dime bag.

"Alicia? Holy shit!" I launched forward and bear-hugged her. It wasn't until I'd pulled back that I clearly saw how different she was from when I'd last seen her. Even her Adam's apple was gone. "Oh my—I wondered when I'd see you again. If."

"I'm sorry," she said. "It's just … I got that new job, and then I had to settle in, and then … other things happened."

"Clearly. How long since—"

"A couple weeks."

"Wait—what? That's all? I thought … with recovery, I mean …"

She smiled, turned around, and lifted the bob of her black hair so that I could see the arrowhead scar at the base of her neck, still a little red from being so recently sutured.

"Come on," she said, striding confidently into my apartment. "I'll tell you all about it."

We talked and smoked for hours. Along with a hefty salary increase, Alicia had acquired an incredible—and incredibly progressive—insurance package that covered, among other things, full synthetic production and additional gender reassignment.

"They didn't flinch when I told them what I needed," she said, proudly. "They gave me the paperwork and told me they'd see me again when I'd finished readjusting to my new skin."

"Weird, it's like they're treating you like a person."

"I know. Shocking."

"Scandalous, even." I pulled out my phone. "Have you spoken to Neesha yet? They'll want to say hi."

"Don't," she said, as I was in the middle of typing out a text.

"What? Why?" I put my phone away.

Alicia shook her head. "Went down that road already. Didn't go so well."

"What do you mean?"

She reached into her purse and pulled out a flat black box, which she passed to me. "I tried taking them a peace offering. It came free with my procedure, but I didn't need it because, well ..."

I stared at the box and the image of the filtration bracelet on the face of it.

"Oh no," I said.

Alicia nodded. "I didn't think ... I mean, I knew they were reticent about this sort of stuff, but ..." She exhaled through her nose. "Anyway, it's yours if you want it. I can even hook you up with a freelance avatar designer."

I cradled the box in both hands. "Thanks, but I'm not sure I fit the bill. I mean, I'm curious, I just ..."

"It's not just for trans and fluid people, you know." She paused. "We're different, you and I, but I understand what it's like not to be seen how you want to be. Maybe this will help you to figure things out."

"But I have figured things out."

She checked her phone. "Look, it's late, and I really need to get going." She stood up. "Let me know if you want to give it a try, okay? I'll put you in touch with my guy. Later," she said, and was gone.

▼ ▼

It was insulting, what she'd implied—that I didn't really know who I was, that this device would suddenly crystalize everything for me or cauterize some open wound of dysphoria I hadn't fully acknowledged. I'd always thought that Alicia got it, that she understood me better than my own family. But she was just like so many others, expecting me to pick a side, as if being non-binary was akin to political centrism.

I put the box on my bathroom counter and went to bed. The next morning, standing in front of the mirror again, pulling myself into tiny, decontextualized pieces, the device within my periphery … before I knew it, I'd opened the box and the smaller jewellery case within.

Inside were the bracelet itself, nestled firmly in a foam impression, and a small chip inside a clear casing no larger than a capsule. I slipped the cold bracelet on my wrist and turned to the mirror again, and like I had so many times before, imagined myself not as one or the other but something in between, something altogether … androgynous. Something at once soft and hard, a person built to no clear specification.

"It creeps me out when you do that," Daneesha had once said to me over drinks at the Railway Club.

"When I do what?"

"When you talk about yourself as if you're … I don't know, a robot or something. A thing manufactured to a set of plans."

It was how I sometimes felt, I told her. Like I hadn't been properly pieced together. Like I was a Lego set built not from one set or another but by combining two or three.

"So what," Daneesha said, "you're some sort of androgynous chimera?"

I'd shrugged in response. "Sometimes, sure." What I didn't tell them was that sometimes it was the only way I could make sense of myself. The only way to justify curves and softness in my body that I couldn't otherwise eradicate.

That afternoon, I called Alicia and told her to put me in touch with her guy.

Her guy, I discovered the next day, was her older brother, Ronnie Chen, whom I'd not seen since we were kids.

"Well, fuck me with a fence post," he said as I entered his North Shore lab on the twelfth floor of a tower overlooking Burrard Inlet and the Lions Gate Bridge. "Sis told me to expect a surprise today."

We sat down, and I explained what I wanted.

"You sound worried," he said. "Like you're going to pick the wrong item off the rack."

"Kind of?"

He swivelled in his seat and went to his computer. Brought up a screen that looked like a super intricate version of a character build screen in a video game, only far more realistic in its options. "You don't have to be," he said. "This isn't a one-and-done sort of thing. There's enough storage space on the bracelet for a handful of identities, should you so desire."

He had me stand on a small circular platform in the centre of the lab. "Keep your arms inside the circle," he said. The perimeter started to glow an intense blue. "And three, two, one. Okay, you can step off now."

I returned to my seat and watched as Ronnie brought up a three-dimensional version of my body, still writing itself into existence. The rendering was naked in the glorified character creator. I wanted to cover myself up, as if I were shielding the other me.

We spent the next hour playing with the various sliders for shape, size, hair, eye colour, stopping and saving every time we settled on an avatar that I liked. I can't say now if, looking at them—at me as them—they felt like *me* or not, but then, I'm still not sure what that's supposed to feel like. When all was said and done, I'd settled on six avatars that I liked, covering both ends of the binary and a fair bit in between—all starting with the root version of me, but shifted in myriad ways. Next, Ronnie took the capsule and inserted it into a small cube-shaped device with a narrow opening on one side. A light on the cube blinked red several times before blinking green, after which point he removed the capsule again.

"It's all yours," he said, handing it to me.

I held the tiny thing in my palm. "What do I do with it?"

"Take it to your GP. Have them schedule the procedure for you. It's outpatient—shouldn't take more than a few minutes to insert it."

"That's not alarming in any way."

"Stelarc would be proud."

"Who?"

"Aren't you studying art?" Ronnie shook his head.

"Anyway," I said, "about this procedure, roughly how much does it cost?"

"I'm not sure, but your insurance should cover it."

"Right. Sooo …"

Ronnie sighed. "How much have you got?"

I opened my wallet, scared that a moth might fly out. "About $225 and change enough for the SkyTrain."

He sighed again and pressed a button on the underside of his desk. Instantly, the blinds lowered. "I should not fucking be doing this," he muttered as I put my money on the desk. He got out of his chair and grabbed what looked like a hypodermic needle, but with a much-fucking-wider circumference and a propellant on the end. "I haven't got any anaesthetic," he said as he loaded the capsule into the syringe and circled around to the back of my chair. He grabbed me by the chin suddenly, pulled my head back, jammed the needle right up my nose and shot what felt like a block of ice into my brain and—

▼ ▼

I came to ten minutes later, a small puddle of drool on my shirt and a trail of mostly dried blood from my nose to my upper lip. Ronnie sat across from me, counting his money.

"Good, you're awake." He spoke without looking up. "I was worried I'd have to roll you up in a rug and dump your body in the river."

"Hello to you, too," I groaned. My whole body felt stiff, like the day after an especially strenuous workout.

Ronnie pocketed the cash and slid the bracelet across the table. "You're all set."

I slipped the bracelet onto my left wrist while waiting for the elevator outside his lab. The purple band of light orbiting its centre started to glow, but nothing felt any different. The elevator doors opened, and I stepped inside. In the mirrors that lined its walls, I saw myself reflected dozens of times in regression. I exhaled, then watched as the ripple happened in real time. My body shimmered and changed, my midsection appearing to crunch inward, giving my torso the illusion of having more muscle. I went to touch myself, but found that my hand stopped at what looked like empty space. It was a reminder: the illusion only went so far. I thought harder about what I wanted to see for myself and watched as, again, my body rippled in place. My hips softened, my hair grew long and fell down my back, and my cheekbones and jaw decreased in prominence. My clothes changed as well—Ronnie had installed several catalogues' worth of potential outfit combinations, for all events and eventualities. When I looked down, I found myself wearing a light summer skirt and a T-shirt that hugged my new curves in a way I'd not previously found comfortable.

And I liked it.

▼ ▼

The fidelity was like nothing I'd ever seen. I spent much of the week that followed watching my changing body, admiring it up close for any dip in the Glamour's resolution, but found nothing that would unintentionally reveal what was beneath whichever shell I decided to wear.

Saturday night, as I was getting ready to put my Glamour to the test, there was an attack. A group of torch- and hatchet-wielding motherfuckers with *God hates trannies* signs and Nazi symbols on their clothing—as unholy a union as ever could be—tore up a downtown club, targeting a group of newts: neutrals, synths who'd altered their new skins to appear genderless and without identifiable ethnicity. They were different shades of grey and together resembled a storm cloud given life. The newts, their attackers claimed, were an affront to decency. They were spitting in the face of what was right, what was natural. I watched a video of the attack, putting my phone away at the first sight of blood.

I met Daneesha an hour later. Right away, they saw the bracelet on my wrist.

"Alicia," they said, crestfallen. "That bitch."

I recoiled. "Look, I know how you feel about this. But just because you don't like it doesn't mean I have to follow suit."

They turned red. "You haven't listened to a word I've said, have you?"

"Neesh—"

"No." They backed away from me. "This"—they pointed to the bracelet—"is nothing more than a bandage for people who don't want to put in the effort to understand us. It's a—"

"A salve, I know, you've given me this speech before."

"Yeah, and it didn't fucking take, did it?"

I felt as if I were suddenly under an interrogation lamp. I wanted nothing more than to crawl out of my skin and disappear. Daneesha saw it then—the ripple as my body's appearance altered itself right in front of them. They watched, stopping mid-rant as I flashed between identities before settling back into my standard issue.

"Look," I said, "I just want to see myself how I want to be seen."

"You mean how you want others to see you. And no, you can't difference-of-opinion your way out of this."

"And you can't tell me how to experience my own body!"

Daneesha scoffed, turned their head, and crossed their arms.

"No, fuck this petulant parent-knows-best bullshit," I continued. "You don't like this. *Fine*. I get it. But you do *not* get to instruct others on how to navigate ... fucking all of this," I said, gesturing wildly. "I don't care if it's a simple fix, it's still a fix. It's *help*, Neesha, and I don't know why you can't see that." I paused. "Or maybe it's that you won't."

They turned back, knifed me with their eyes. "Really? You're going to go there?"

"You already went there. I'm not going to let you walk all over me because you feel ... iffy about this. This"—I raised my wrist in the air—"can be as much a part of who I am as anything. That's my decision to make, not yours or anyone else's."

Their glare intensified, nothing but fire and ire. "'Iffy'? *Iffy*? The fuck is wrong with you? It isn't real!"

"That's not for you to decide!"

Disgusted, Daneesha dismissed me with a wave and turned to leave. I ran after them.

"Neesha, I don't understand, what the hell have I done that's so wrong? Just ... why can't I have this for myself?"

They shook their head. "You don't—seeing you like this ... it hurts. It feels ... I don't know, like you're making fun of me."

I stepped back. "I'd never. This has nothing to do with you. I just ... I need to know. For me."

Their face softened, anger still evident but less volcanic. "You know this won't solve anything, right? It's just another way to hide, as if you needed help with that. You need to embrace who you really are."

"Easier said than done. You don't know what it's like to spend every day dissecting yourself in literally every reflective surface you pass."

"You don't know that I don't."

"Then why don't you get why I want this?"

"Because." They reached out, fondled the bracelet. For a second I thought they were going to yank it right off. "You're acting like a tourist, trying on bodies that aren't yours. That's not progress, Sister Hyde. It's not right."

"'That aren't mine'? What, you think that being non-binary means I don't get to experiment?"

"Your words, not mine."

"No, fuck that. That's not fucking fair and you know it."

"You're not fluid and you're not trans. Playing like you are is just gross."

"How I define myself is none of your fucking business. And I'm not *playing* like I'm anything."

"Good, 'cause you fucking aren't."

"Fuck off."

"You first."

▼ ▼

The light in my bathroom continued to strobe. I held up a hand mirror, angling it so that it flared directly into the wall-mounted mirror. With the Glamour activated, I riddled myself with bullet holes of light. When I moved, the parallax between the different planes of me created a living exquisite corpse.

I was starting to adapt to the different ways I saw myself. Some days I was an entirely new person, while others I simply tightened up my appearance as if the Glamour were a belt I could cinch around my waist to vanish everything unwanted.

I went out the following Saturday to a club down on Davie, near English Bay. They were having a "new wave" event—synths drank for free. I was a long way from being able to afford a second skin, but I decided to check it out anyway, to see the spectacle of it all.

The place was chaos; the dance floor was dark and teeming with life. Right away, among the synths and other standard-issue meat sacks, I noticed the dangling silver bracelets on many others. Seeing them there felt like spotting kin in the wild, people like me who'd chosen another way, one that didn't require sticking a flag in the sand to any one side. I noticed my own Glamour vacillating between different gender presentations anytime I felt slight pangs of envy for another's body. It was … it was everything.

A man sat close behind me. He had a shaved head and thick black glasses and a tattoo of a coiled snake on the inside of one of his forearms. He ordered a beer, turning to me as the bartender fetched him his drink.

"Nice night," I said.

The guy nodded once, like he was flicking me off with his forehead, and returned to his drink. I got up to leave.

"That make you feel better?" he said suddenly.

"What?"

He pointed the neck of his beer at my wrist. "That make you feel any more whole, freak?"

I hid my wrist behind my back. My shell shimmered but did not crack. He raised an eyebrow, then reached out fast and grabbed my other wrist. Squeezed enough to hurt. My change was so sudden that my field of vision flared white for a full second as my outward appearance shifted male. I clenched up, ready for whatever was next. Terror like fireworks in my brain.

"You mind letting go of me?" I wrestled my arm free and started for the exit, but I was stopped by another man with a similar tattoo blocking the way, occupying the space like a gravestone swollen in size. I looked around then and saw others like them dotting the club's interior like an infection about to fuck up its host.

I turned to the first man. "What are you—"

▼ ▼

I woke on the ground, my head feeling like it had been split in two. Not sure how much time had passed.

I looked around groggily, saw people clutching themselves, waiting for their Glamours to reset, and synths on the ground, all of them face down.

Holes in the backs of their necks. Blood everywhere.

Anti-synth bigots claimed synth lives were immaterial, that they'd already died and were just skin sacks with a hard drive. As if to prove their point, they'd stolen the halos of all the synths there, to wipe them as easily as one would delete a file.

I got out of there before the killers could return. Evidence of their destruction trailed out the back, a dotted line of viscera like the absolute worst *Family Circus* panel.

I kicked something hard then, in the alley behind the club. I looked down. On the pavement, in a splatter of red with bits of tissue clinging to it, was a cerebral slate: a halo. Just a small three-quarter ring of plastic and circuitry that at one point had been someone's entire world.

I picked it up, getting red on me, and looked behind me.

It was someone's.

It was *someone*.

I should go back, I thought. I should wait for the police to arrive. They could take it to Eternia or another extended life clinic and figure out who it belonged to. Who it was.

I should have, but I didn't.

▼ ▼

A trick of the light. That's all it is.

I pick up the bracelet again, broken in the attack, and slip it on, watch as an ill-fitting shell filters overtop, myriad identities fractured and spliced into one chimeric disaster.

To the left of me, the halo is a splotch on the counter. When the light flickers, I don't even see the blood. Just promise. Something to hold on to. A new opportunity—to be someone else, if that's what I want. If it's what I need.

To be more than just a trick of the light.

# CREATURE NOT OF THIS LAGOON

## Anton Pooles

His kicks send pulses down
into the lagoon's underworld

I slither out
from my dark cave
to find him circling above
        Alien? Angel?

Otherworldly creature, I long

to reach out and touch
his scallop-white foot
with my webbed claw

but after one small caress
he fires off
        like a torpedo
for the tramp steamer
leaving me just below the surface

wondering if I could ever pass
through the threshold
between
his world and mine

        or is it safer
in the depths
of my monochromatic
lagoon?

Then I remember the creatures
who came before me

and the Universal stories of
*love leads to destruction*

reject attraction—
*we cannot guarantee your safety*

And if we ever forgot
our place
even for a moment

we were reminded
with a plethora of sequels

# POEM MADE FROM PENNYWISE
David Ly

When I put *It* on
　　　　my jaw relaxes and unclenches
once Bill Skarsgård chomps down to feast

　　on the kids of Derry.
　　　I'm breathing with ease after
I see the demonic clown's grin,

　　　　　my worries and anxieties dissipate
　　without even having to count
　how many balloons are needed
to make It float.

　I've abandoned breathing
　　techniques and listening to ambient noises

　and now stare at anxiety straight in the mouth,

　　razor-sharp teeth
dripping with grey water

until it all drifts away
　　　like a bundle of shiny red balloons

# AND THE MOON SPUN ROUND LIKE A TOP

Hiromi Goto

**BERNADETTE NAKASHIMA POWERED DOWN HER PC** and rolled her chair away from her desk. A small sigh seeped from her lips as she stared down at her short arms. The muscles were so tight that even at rest, her fingers were half-curled. A miniature T. Rex.

She raised her arms above her head as she hopped down from her chair. Hands aloft, she squeezed them into fists, releasing, squeezing, and releasing before dropping her arms to shake out both hands furiously at her hips, her fingers flapping wildly.

"Carpal tunnel?" Mathew Murakami asked sympathetically.

Bernadette went still. She turned her head ninety degrees to her right to gaze at her desk neighbour. The newest auxiliary worker to be wiggled into their department, Mathew was still eager, and his smile excessive. Bernadette realized a little too late that he was being friendly. She modified her lips into a twitch of a smile and shrugged. "You must have weekend plans," she said, and bent to retrieve her purse and rummage for her cellphone. She was only being polite—she had no interest in Mathew's weekend, planned or otherwise. Management would love to nudge her out and have low-cost Mathew take her place.

She was at the top of her pay scale, with seven years remaining before retirement—there was no way she would leave without the security of her pension.

She frowned. It wasn't like Mathew not to respond. Slipping her arm through the handles of her purse, she stood up and faced him once more.

Two spots of red flared on Mathew's wan complexion. What on earth did he have to feel embarrassed about?

"Ummm …"

Bernadette watched, amazed, as the tips of his pale ears began to glow brightly red.

Mathew coughed and then swallowed, his Adam's apple bobbling. "It's …"

"What? Spit it out!" Bernadette snapped. Her heart seized. Had management spoken to him already? They wouldn't dare! Not before speaking with her.

"I think you might want to go to the ladies' room," Mathew whispered. He packed up his desk in seconds and was out the door, leaving behind his suit jacket, before Bernadette had a chance to respond.

She gave her head a little shake. The office was empty. Out in the hallway, a garbage trolley with a misaligned wheel squeaked past, pushed by an office cleaner with oversized headphones.

Frowning, Bernadette glanced down at her herself. Had she spilled salad dressing down her front during lunch? Good god, she hadn't dipped her breast into the little soya sauce dish again, had she—

A warm, soft bulge of blood slid down her vagina. Instinctively Bernadette squeezed the muscles of her nether region, *clenched*, but it was too late. Warmcool trickled down her inner thigh.

She ran, stiff-legged, out of the open space office and down the hall to the unisex single-occupancy washroom, hoping she wasn't leaving a trail behind her. She burst through the door and locked it as she yanked down her slacks. She sat down without bothering to drape paper over the toilet seat.

The crotch of her panties was bright red. The blood clot, solid as a chunk of liver, was the size of a gerbil.

Bernadette bit her lip. Her period shouldn't have started for another five days. And usually there were a few days of watery warning. But perimenopause was wreaking havoc upon her cycles. It'd never been this bad, however.

Her cheeks filled with heat. Mathew had seen her blood. Like she was in junior high school! What did her seniority matter after this?

There was a spare shirt in her locker, which she hadn't opened for over half a year, but she didn't have an extra pair of slacks in there. Nor underwear. And her closest work friend, Glenda John—although they weren't particularly intimate, per se—was long gone, snarled up in the long commute back to Maple Ridge.

Well, there was no undoing it. She would take care of it herself, as she'd always done. Take care of your own business, her mother had hissed at Bernadette and her younger sister when they were growing up. It had been a confusing lesson for a three-year-old, among the many lessons she'd been taught. She hadn't realized how odd her mother was until Bernadette was in high school and allowed a little more freedom, but by then the early imprinting had already taken.

Odd daughter of an odd mother.

She tore some toilet paper from the dispenser, picked out the rodent-sized clot from her panties, and dropped it into the water. She yanked a big wad of paper from the roll and folded it around her gusset and squeezed. There was so much blood that she had to apply paper three more times.

She turned her attention to the crotch of her slacks. The pale-grey cotton-and-poly blend was marked with a dark-red bull's eye with a brown corona. It was the size of a baby's head.

Her mouth compressed tight. She peeled the slacks from her legs, hung them over the door of the stall, then shucked her underpants. She dropped her soiled undergarment into the sanitary napkin disposal unit.

There were arcs of dried blood on the soft flesh of her inner thighs where they rubbed together at her crotch. No point in trying to tidy up her legs. There'd only be more blood. She rolled up a thick cushion of toilet paper and wadded it into the crotch of her pants, pulling them up as high as the elastic waist would go. She squeezed her inner thighs together to try to lock the wad in place. She flushed the toilet.

The water swirled a sluggish pink, overwhelmed with all the paper. Dread filled Bernadette's esophagus. Would she cause a flood on top of everything else? The toilet belched as it swallowed the bloody mass. Relieved, she waddled to the hallway.

At her locker, she swirled through the numbers of the lock—after several tries it released with a *clack*.

There wasn't a shirt, after all, but a navy-blue cardigan. She could tie it around her bottom like a wraparound skirt. Like that troubled Kennedy woman had done in the documentary *Grey Gardens* so long ago—she had made it look elegant, somehow. Bernadette was by no means an elegant lady, but it would do. She would call a cab. An extravagance, but sometimes such things were necessary.

▼ ▼

Providence, pragmatism's love child, had left a yogurt tub of frozen beef and barley soup in the freezer. Her mother had been a fount of idioms she'd made up on her own. Bernadette had not known that they were originals until she'd started using them in conversation when she was older. People found them quirky and hilarious for some reason, so she kept them in her repertoire and pulled them out whenever she was obligated to attend a work social function.

She lay down upon her couch while she waited for her supper to warm. She frowned at her bare feet sticking out of her pyjama bottoms. They were not attractive.

She'd put a giant nighttime pad inside two pairs of underwear, but she could tell that the blood had stopped flowing from the way her tender parts chafed dryly against the pad.

A yawn cracked her face so wide it almost hurt. She shouldn't feel this tired. She'd been getting plenty of sleep, especially since quitting social media half a year ago. Her slacks—she should run water through the blood before the stain set. They weren't an expensive pair, but they were her most comfortable. But Bernadette's eyelids were so heavy. They drooped. Opened. Closed, a sinking sweet, slow drop …

*Bleat! Bleat! Bleat! Bleat!*

The sound of the smoke alarm had her heart plugging her throat. Acrid smoke. She coughed as she rolled off the couch, staggered to the kitchen window, and shoved it open. Rain gusted inward, a wet pelting upon her face. She spun to the stove—the element was a dull red, the bottom of the pot scorched, plastic handle sagging from the heat, black smoke roiling above it. Bernadette snatched up a pot holder, grabbed the base of the handle, ran to the open window, and tossed everything out her third-storey apartment.

The red-hot pot screamed with the sudden change in temperature, a huge hiss of steam rising upward as it plummeted to the wet shrubbery below. Bernadette ducked under her window ledge, as if sheltering herself from grenades.

*Oh, my.* Her heart's painful mallet: Oh dear, oh dear.

*Thud! Thud! Thud!*

She shrieked and tears began streaming from her eyes.

"Miss Bernadette!" a voice called out. "Miss Bernadette, are you okay?"

It was Timo, the building caretaker. He lived in the apartment below hers. A great convenience when the sink plugged over the weekend, but at a time like this? What if he'd seen the steaming pot fly past his balcony? She couldn't say she'd fallen asleep with the stove on—could they evict her for such a thing?

She flapped a tea towel at the smoky air, trying to force it toward the open window. The smoke alarm continued bleating. Timo pounded at the door. Bernadette grabbed the broom and prodded at the alarm.

The cover fell off. She poked at the mechanism until the battery popped out and the bleating stopped. She ran to the front door and opened it.

Timo, a little dishevelled in navy-blue sweatpants and a red-checkered flannel shirt, stood with his fist still raised to knock upon the door, a frown of concern etched on his face. He couldn't have been too many years younger than she was, but he spoke to her as if she were elderly, someone who couldn't work the remote of a new television.

"Miss Bernadette," Timo said, his eyes darting past her face to the smokiness of her apartment. "Are you okay? Is there a fire?"

"It's nothing. Everything's fine!" Bernadette smiled. "Thank you for your concern, Timo. I spilled something on a burner, and it burnt to a crisp. But there was no danger."

Timo stared at her, and Bernadette realized that her cheeks were wet. She swiped at her face with the back of her hand. "I opened the window to clear the air, and the rain ..." Hot tears surged in the back of her throat, and she blinked rapidly to ward against them. "Never mind!"

Timo nodded, raising both hands, palms forward. "I'm glad you're fine," he said softly. "Good night, Miss Bernadette." He turned away, disappearing through the hallway door.

A small knot of guilt sat in Bernadette's belly. Disliking the sensation, she shut the door with more force than required. The thud echoed.

In the kitchen, a gust of rain rattled the half-closed blinds. Bernadette ran and slammed the window shut. "Horrible," she whispered. It was 9:47 p.m. She was desperately hungry. And so very tired.

An aura of heat warmed her back. It felt nice.

She spun around. The element on the stove glowed beautifully red—a shade so saturated that it made a person want to touch it. She vigorously shook her head. Clicked the burner off. Double-checked the other burners. Off. Off. Off. Unplugged her low-tech rice cooker and kettle, just to be certain.

Her eyes wandered over her modest home. Tasteful. Bookshelves made of oak. An outdated CD player. Two orchids, one in bloom, one not. In the kitchen a bitter smell still hovered in the air. She plucked the first takeout menu she saw from the odds and ends drawer. Bernadette rarely ordered take-away, but whenever her younger sister, Agnes, came for one of her rare visits, she enjoyed ordering in. A medium artichoke and olive pizza, Bernadette decided, adding an unwanted Greek salad so that the delivery would be free.

▼ ▼

The weekend passed without any further upset. Her menstrual flow had dried up to nothing, her exhaustion replaced by pizza-induced indigestion. On Sunday she allowed herself a walk around Lost Lagoon at Stanley Park. The arched necks and partially raised wings of the mute swans filled Bernadette's heart with a feeling so fierce she couldn't name it. On her way home, she stopped at International Village to look at the cashmere sweaters, the winter items on sale. But the prices were just a bit much, and the sweater she bought five years ago was still serviceable. Maybe next year.

Bernadette caught her reflection in the mirror. She quickly turned away. Do I really look like that? She was always surprised to see herself outside of her home or office.

She glanced at her watch, then gazed up at the ceiling of the cashmere store. On the top floor of the mall was a movie theatre that screened second-run films. She hadn't watched a film in a theatre for ages.

One film was starting in ten minutes: *The Babadook*. Bernadette knew nothing about it. The poster didn't give that much away, although there was something a little unpleasant about the silhouette of the top-hatted figure with spiky whiskers and fingers—it reminded her of that author Sendak's picture books. A little dark. Was it a film for young people? The film was rated 14A. Well, if a fourteen-year-old could watch it, certainly she could, as well. She bought her ticket and entered the theatre, delighted to discover it mostly empty. She plunked herself down in the middle of the middle and turned her face toward the screen, the flicker of lights, and the swelling thunder of Dolby surround.

▼ ▼

The night had turned cold. A few stars glinted in the flat sky above the city, and Bernadette pulled the lapels of her wool coat snugly against her throat as she walked along the sidewalk toward the bus stop. That film … The film had left her feeling dry in the mouth, a little sick to her stomach. It wasn't the sort of story she liked, not at all. And now it was well and dark. Back to work tomorrow, and uneasiness pressing upon her chest like the weight of a cat. She shuddered. That was what happened when you decided to do something on a whim, without enough research. You ended up watching something you'd rather have left unseen.

Cars roared past at the change of lights, and Bernadette picked up her pace, her shoes clacking against the pavement. She felt awful for that poor woman in the story. Even after feminism had roared so fiercely in the seventies, it was no picnic. All that responsibility on her fragile shoulders, and a child who was a little touched. The poor things. Bernadette shook her head. She herself had vowed never to be a single mother. She knew she wouldn't be able to handle it all on her own. Some women could and did so admirably, but she was not one of those women. And, what with her odd ways, her preference for her own company and a good book at home, romantic relationships had dried up by the time she hit the latter part of her thirties.

Her regrets were few. And she thanked her lucky stars she had never been trapped into unwanted motherhood.

"Hey!" a rough voice called.

Bernadette's heart leapt. She glanced over her shoulder.

A man in a heavy coat, a baseball cap pulled low over his face, was half a block behind her, walking in the same direction. He staggered a little with a kind of lurch to each step, as if the ground heaved beneath his feet. Like he might be drunk.

Bernadette cast wildly about. They were the only two pedestrians. A few cars and trucks passed them. She glanced over her shoulder again. The man had drawn a little closer.

A patch of yellow behind him. Moving toward them.

"Taxi!" Bernadette shouted. She raised her hand and waved it frantically in the air. "Taxi!"

The taxi came to a stop beside her, and she opened the door with a trembling hand and jumped inside.

"Hey!" the man shouted. "What time is it? I just wanted to know the time, you stupid bitch!"

Bernadette slammed the door shut. "Go," she said curtly. "Please."

"You okay?" the taxi driver asked. His electric car silently accelerated.

"I'm fine," Bernadette said, as tears streamed down her face. "He just wanted to know the time."

When she arrived at home, she took a hot shower, brushed her teeth, and went straight to bed. She pulled the blanket, the edge of it held tight in two fists, up over her mouth, leaving her nose uncovered. She blinked in the darkness, listening to the rattle of a shopping cart travel along the back alley. The clack of garbage bins opening and closing as bottle collectors made their nightly rounds.

Her heart dropped.

Her office chair. She'd left her menstrual blood to set in the grey polyester fabric. All weekend long. And now it would never come out. Out, out, damned spot. Her heart began a heavy thudding inside her chest, the sensation filling her with dread. As dark and unrelenting as the Babadook …

*Stop it! You can go to the office early and deal with it. You're not in junior high school. Don't be ridiculous. Breathe slowly. Exhale. Nobody cares,* she told herself. *Nobody cares except you. It's okay. Don't worry. Nobody cares.*

▼ ▼

The hallway was empty. Forty minutes before official start time was early enough on a Monday to avoid running into anyone. Bernadette sighed with relief as she thrust a pair of trousers, a sweater, and a shirt into her locker. Atop the clothes, she placed a paper bag of spare underwear, tampons, and heavy-flow nighttime pads with wings. She would never be caught unprepared again.

She clanged the door shut and spun the lock with satisfaction. Now to deal with the chair.

Before leaving home, she'd forced a regular-sized tampon into her dry vagina. Walking made it scrape painfully against her tender flesh. She grimaced with discomfort as she opened the door to the large open-office space.

There, beside her desk, more than thirty-five minutes before the official start time, sat Mathew.

Bernadette's heart hammered inside her ears. Her breath grew shallow. *I hate you …*

Mathew turned around as if he'd heard her and gave her a little half wave. She could see the red burn in his ears even from twenty feet away.

Bernadette held her shoulders high. She never would have thought of Mathew as a cruel person. But to shame her in this way? She marched toward him in her flat work shoes, a thin smile on her lips. Well, so be it.

"You're here early," she said. "Preparing for the meeting this afternoon?"

"Morning," Mathew said. Even seated, he was almost eye level to her. His eyes nervously slid off her face, and she watched, distastefully, as his Adam's apple bobbled. His next words came in a fast, breathy whisper: "I-took-your-chair-to-supplies-and-brought-back-a-new-one." He turned to his computer. A mechanical *bong* rang out as its old engine began to whir. He stared fixedly at the blue screen as the beach ball spun.

Bernadette whipped her head toward her desk.

It was true. The chair was new and the seat spotless. It also had armrests. Her old one had not. She had chosen a chair without arm-rests because the rests were positioned incorrectly for her short height and not useful to her in any way.

Relief, gratitude, and resentment roiled inside of her. Who asked Mathew to interfere in her affairs? By "helping" he was drawing more attention to the entire ignoble incident, adding a second layer of shame. And then placing her in a position of having to *thank him* for it all.

Why couldn't people leave her alone? She left everyone else alone.

She sat in her new chair and faced her desktop computer. She turned it on and watched the beach ball spin. She could feel heat emanating from Mathew's head and the weight of the silence between them.

They clattered their keyboards as they worked through the emails in their inboxes, which never cleared. They worked furiously and silently until the rest of their workmates began trickling in, bringing with them the pinched, sour smell of cheap coffee.

When Sasha came up to Mathew's desk to ask him if he'd gone to the Jesse the K concert at the Commodore over the weekend, Mathew's relief was so great it almost sounded like a sob.

"How was your weekend?" Glenda John asked.

Bernadette looked up. Of all the people she knew, Glenda John was the only one who had never tried to hug her. Glenda referred to herself as queer, which Bernadette didn't really understand. At a Christmas party three years ago, someone who had had too much to drink had told Bernadette that even though she might not be gay, jeez was she ever queer.

"Peaceful," Bernadette said. "And yours?"

"Ohhh," Glenda John said, "it's been interesting."

Bernadette glanced at her officemate's face. Was this the moment she was meant to pry into Glenda John's personal life?

Glenda John gave a wry grin and moved toward her desk pod.

Bernadette's heart swelled with appreciation. Glenda John was a decent individual. If only there were more like her in the world.

Meanwhile, Mathew had been chattering non-stop about the stunning bass player at the concert, his sentences punctuated by bursts of nervous laughter. Bernadette could see Sasha trying to inch away from him.

The office finally settled into a low hum: the constant clatter of keyboards, the murmur of modulated voices talking on the phone. Bernadette wriggled in her chair. It was a little too high, and her knees were becoming sore, the weight of her feet and calves hanging from her ball-and-socket hinges. She clicked her tongue. The discomfort was growing, and she could already feel her ankles swelling. She'd never make it until coffee break, and now she'd have to fiddle with the seat while everyone was still around. And all on account of Mathew. She awkwardly lowered herself from the chair and crouched beside the large plastic screw in the back that adjusted the height of the seat.

The tampon she'd forced into her dry vagina shot out like a greased bullet. She froze.

From her crouched position, Bernadette slowly stood up, as carefully as she could. Legs straightened, she bent over at the waist under some notion that doing so would help. Headfirst, she ran across the open office floor. The bloated and slick tampon slid about in her loose underpants, and she could feel a large clot nudging against her inner labia. She ran like a battering ram.

As she burst out into the hallway, a sound swelled behind her, starting low, then growing, like a wave.

Laughter. Everyone. Laughing.

They were laughing at her.

Rage was a red-hot coal in her throat. The gleeful pitch of it—as if they'd been waiting, all this time, to have a *reason* to laugh at her. She banged open the door to the single-occupancy bathroom and slammed it shut. Clicked the lock. Thumbed down her slacks and sat on the toilet and wept.

She didn't know how long the discreet tapping had been going on before she finally noticed it. She grabbed toilet paper and blew her nose, wiped her face. "Yes," she said. That didn't sound so bad, she thought.

"Is there anything I can get you?" Glenda John asked.

A hot surge of tears filled Bernadette's eyes once more. Of course Glenda John wouldn't ask ridiculous questions like *Are you okay?* She could almost fall in love with someone like Glenda John. "Actually, yes." Bernadette cleared her throat. "I have some spare pants in my locker, and a brown paper bag. Could bring them to me, please? You can just leave it by the door." She told Glenda John the locker code and sat back on the seat with a sigh.

Bernadette's eyes dropped to the crotch of her underwear. Nestled beside the useless, bloated tampon was a blood clot the size of a full-grown hamster.

When she had first started producing big blood clots, she'd gone online and discovered that it was normal, that clots ranged in size and consistency, especially during "the change." But this? Was this *normal*? Not only was it the size of a hamster, it almost looked like one, with four stubby limb-like protrusions. A rounded bulge that was almost a head …

She grimaced with disgust and fascination. Then bent over to get a better look at the jellylike consistency, a bright, deep ruby. It glistened inside her soiled clothing like a jewel. She stretched out her forefinger and gave it a little nudge.

The blood clot recoiled from her touch.

Bernadette's heart stopped.

*Tap, tap, tap.*

She swallowed a scream. She clamped her hand over her mouth as her heart pounded inside her ears.

"Here's your stuff," Glenda John said from the hallway. "I went ahead and brought your purse and jacket, too. You could just take a sick day, if you wanted. That's what I'd do."

"Thank you," Bernadette whispered, as she continued staring at the clot. "You can leave it on the floor." She heard a small thump. Glenda John's Merrells squidged away from the door.

Bernadette had only imagined that the lump of blood had moved, of course. Because it was so wet and shiny. *She* had moved, and the reflected light had shimmered—

The dark clot humped and squirmed, humped and squirmed like a plump red grub on the sticky surface of her gusset.

Bernadette quelled her shriek. She bit down, swallowed, and the displaced force made her eyes bulge against her eyelids.

How was it possible? How could it be? It wasn't a fetus, because she hadn't had sex for over nine years! Could she have gone out unconsciously, had sex, then come home without ever knowing?

She shook her head. Preposterous!

*Plop.*

The clot of blood sank into the toilet bowl. Rings of red expanded on the surface of the water as the flayed hamster drifted to the bottom.

Bernadette stared, mouth open. It squirmed, flip-flopped, twisted, and stretched. *It must feel the cold*, she thought. *It will die soon. Just flush it. Out of sight, out of mind.*

She knelt beside the toilet bowl. A whiff of vomit rising from the folds of the rim. Her hand plunged into the water, fingers outstretched. She sieved through the bowl until she felt the fleshy snag against her skin. The movement was feeble, like a dying tadpole. She rotated her hand palm upward, forming a small bowl, and gently lifted that living part of her out of the dirty water.

Half propped out of the garbage receptacle in the wall was a paper cup. Bernadette staggered to her feet, pressing the edge of her cupped hand against her belly to protect the contents of her palm. With her free hand, she grabbed the paper cup, set it on the counter, then turned on both faucets. She rinsed out the rime of coffee, then filled it half-full with warm water. Gently, she tipped the lump of blood inside.

It slowly drifted to the bottom.

Motionless.

She gently jostled the cup, pitching the water from side to side. The blood clot rocked with the water's motion.

Bernadette bit her lip. What in the world was she *doing*?

What did it matter? She wasn't doing anything wrong. It was her own body, after all! Wasn't she just being curious about her own body? Wasn't that called science?

She carefully tipped the water out of the cup, leaving just a thin lining of liquid in the bottom. So that the clot wouldn't dry out.

She would take it home. She wanted to look at it a little more closely. And maybe she ought to take it to her doctor.

She set the cup on the counter and tidied herself up. Retrieved the fresh clothes Glenda John had left for her outside the door. After rustling through wads of wet paper towels in the garbage, she found the lid for the coffee cup. She popped it back on and nestled the container inside her purse, beside her wallet and Day-timer. She left work without saying a thing.

▼ ▼

Bernadette stared at the blood lump inside the large glass jar. In her other hand, she held the spray bottle she used for her orchids just above the opening.

The dull red clot remained motionless. She must have imagined seeing it move, she decided—the result of heightened emotions. She blinked rapidly, a flurry of lashes and uneasiness. She pulled the lever on the nozzle. *Fsssssst*. A fine mist of water fell into the jar atop the inert blob.

*Fsssssst. Fsssssst.*

It quivered.

Bernadette gasped. With both hands, she slowly raised the jar level with her eyes.

The raw lump arched its back, then stretched forward, arched and stretched, just like an inchworm, until it ringed the entire circumference of the jar.

Proof! Evidence! Bernadette gently set the jar on the kitchen floor and stumbled to her purse. She found her cellphone and staggered back, flicking the screen, then tapping in her password. She flicked to the video setting and pressed record.

*Go on. Don't be like that singing and dancing frog in the cartoon!* Because she needed proof, didn't she? Proof that she wasn't imagining things.

Her hand shook as she held the cellphone in front of her, trying to centre the blood creature in the middle of the screen. Her hand was jittering so much it was impossible to tell if the thing was moving. On screen, one could scarcely make out what it was. She needed a tripod. Or whatever one used to steady a cellphone. How could she—

A hot, round bulge billowed through her vagina.

It was big. Bigger than anything she'd ever felt before. She set down her cellphone and cupped her hand around her vulva. She ran for the bathroom. No time to turn on the lights. She shucked her pyjama bottoms, but instead of sitting on the toilet, she grabbed the wash basin from her tub and crouched above it.

The malleable mass conformed to the size of her canal, scarcely stretching her at all. It slid out, slick and easy. "Oh god," Bernadette cried, "oh god!" The enormous clump splooped out from between her labia and fell into the wash basin with a wet splat.

All Bernadette could think was: liver. She was birthing her own organs. Look! She'd given birth to her own liver! Wasn't that a scream!

In the darkness of the unlit washroom, a pale light seeping from down the hall and the open kitchen, the mass of blood looked black. It was as large as a peeled guinea pig. She hefted the weight of it in her palms. Easily two pounds, she thought. *Two pounds! Came out of me!*

Not her liver. It was that … thing. They'd talked about it on the college radio program. The thing some women got. Fibres—fibroids!

Warm tears filled her eyes and spilled down her face. She sank to the floor as relief sapped away the adrenalin-fuelled tension.

*It's only fibroids.* A smile trembled on her lips. *You silly goose!* She gave the basin a little shake and laughed aloud. She'd book an appointment with her overly young doctor and call in sick tomo—

The giant clot of blood squealed.

Bernadette clamped her hands over her ears. The basin fell flat upon the floor. The rodent clot continued shrieking—a piercing pitch, like it was being slowly stabbed with a long, thin needle.

She had to stop the noise! Timo's apartment was directly beneath hers. Oh, she should have thought it through more carefully when she'd moved into the building six years ago. The caretaker of the building, who lived where he worked—he was practically a spy. She grabbed a towel from the rack and tumbled the cloth around the two-pound clot, wrapping it tight, muffling it.

The shrieking stopped.

Just the flutter of her heartbeat inside her ears. Bernadette took a long, shuddering pull of air deep into her lungs.

A quiet mewing. Not from the lump wrapped up in the towel in her hands. It was coming from the kitchen.

She stared out from the darkened room toward the dim stream of light that crept down the hallway.

"*Mew, mew, mew,*" the blood hamster in the jar cried.

The warm lump in her hands quivered. A churning, twisting, writhing. The nubbly cloth fell away, and Bernadette was cupping the flayed guinea pig in her bare palms, sticky wet, the rich and thick odour of blood.

A sharp pain punched through her forefinger, the fleshy part below the first joint. Bernadette gasped.

Sucking. She could feel the suction, the painful throb of her broken flesh. The wet sounds of swallowing.

The raw guinea pig. It was hungry ...

They were hungry.

What manner of life was this?

*My very cells.* A stunted laugh erupted from her lips. Startled by the noise, the bloody guinea pig stopped sucking for a moment, then began feeding more strongly, as if worried its sustenance would be taken away.

"What am I supposed to do?" Bernadette asked.

"*Mew,*" cried the little one from the jar in the kitchen. "*Mew, mew, mew.*"

*It must be even hungrier than this one,* Bernadette thought dimly. She slowly rose to her feet and shuffled toward the kitchen, carefully carrying the feeding clot with her. Grey afternoon light fell upon it. It seemed to flinch, pull away a little from the finger it was sucking. But it didn't loosen its grip. The pain burned.

The toothed clot that nursed from her finger looked very much like the hamster clot, only it was much bigger. A kind of translucent flesh-iness, with darker strands of varying widths striping the body. They looked like veins. It had little stumpy limbs like its hamster sibling. But it had no face. No eyes.

And yet it had a mouth for eating. Teeth for biting.

Maybe it was a tumour, Bernadette thought. A tumour with teeth. "That's not nice," she said. Clearly this sort of thing required medical help. Obviously. She ought to call 911. People could help her. That was their job.

But this was not a normal thing. And she would not be treated like a normal person. She would be treated as an object. They would measure. And take photographs. Pry and prod. Once she agreed to their procedures, she gave up her autonomy, and her body was not her own. *How disgusting,* she thought. Whatever the medical profession examined, it owned. And what would become of her private life then? In this age of instant notoriety?

"No!" Bernadette shouted. She took a deep breath. No. No one would make a spectacle of her life.

The mewling of the little lump in the jar grew softer, a whisper of a cry. The large one in her hands continued feeding from her finger. It wasn't taking much of her blood—not like it was tapped into an artery. But, really, how long could she feed it this way?

The little one had gone silent. Had she killed it? Because she hadn't known how to care for it? She crouched down beside the jar. The little one seemed to have lost its shape. The stumpy little limbs no longer protruded, and it was flat upon the cold glass. A pale, pinkish liquid streaked the circular seam of the jar's circumference.

*Maybe it's just lonely*, she thought.

Grimacing, she curled her thumb and forefinger around the body of the flayed guinea pig still suckling from her other hand. She squeezed gently and prised it forward slightly, against the downward hook of its small teeth. *Just like unhooking a brassiere*, she thought. The bloody guinea pig came off her finger with a soft suction pop.

It dangled from her grip, its four stubby limbs waving uselessly. It smelled clean and fresh, not like the heavy-smelling old blood at the end of her menstrual cycle.

She carefully worked it through the opening of the jar and set it down beside the little blood that had gone so still. They were nestled beside each other. The larger one blindly raised its faceless "head" and bobbed here and there, as if seeking, or smelling the air. Bernadette peered through the side of the jar, the distortive curve of the glass.

The fleshy guinea pig bit into the hamster.

The smaller blood clot gave a final quiver, then began to shrink to the sounds of persistent sucking. The striated veins on the larger clot surged and shrank in time with its feeding.

Bernadette inched backwards. She scooted on her bum through the doorway and sat, arms clamped around her knees, in the hallway, staring at the jar in the middle of the kitchen floor.

*Cannibal*, she thought. *My body … part of me … is a cannibal.*

She staggered to the washroom and heaved into the toilet bowl. But nothing came out. She'd eaten nothing.

She flicked on the light and ran hot water at the sink. She raised her forefinger to her eyes. The puncture wound was small—not round holes left by pointed teeth, but two small horizontal lines. Her flesh was a little white around the cuts, as if she'd spent too long in the bathtub. She opened the medicine cabinet and retrieved the hydrogen peroxide. Awkwardly, she poured it over her wound.

A flutter inside her vagina. Nudge, nudging at her vulva.

Hot tears rolled down Bernadette's face.

▼ ▼

She could not say how many skinless creatures she had passed during the long night. After running out of jars, soup pots, bowls, and basins, she'd risked a dash to the dark alley, where she found a cat carrier, some old Tupperware containers, and, of all things, a discarded baby's bathtub.

From the kitchen and living room rose a constant ebb and flow of clicks and squeals, chitterings and hums. Intermittent shrieks pierced the air.

Bernadette lay flat in the bottom of her bathtub, her knees raised into two triangles, her lower half naked. With no heat vent in the room, she had grown colder and colder as she passed clot after clot of varying size. Until she realized the heat lamp in the ceiling could keep her warm.

The heat lamp felt like sunshine against her closed eyelids.

*How can I still be alive?* If she gathered all of the blood animals and weighed them, they would equal her weight.

Hunger roared in her belly. But the pizza and Chinese food she might order now, in the middle of the night, didn't have enough iron. The thought of the old iron pills in her cupboard made her want to retch. She needed meat. Saliva filled her mouth at the thought of bloody steak. When the grocery store opened in the morning, she would order ten pounds—no, twenty pounds of steak to be delivered.

The noise from the kitchen and living room was too loud. Maybe if the animals filled up on blood, they would quiet and fall asleep.

*Knock, knock, knock.*

"Miss Bernadette," Timo's voice called from the other side of the door.

Bernadette held her breath. Maybe if she didn't respond, he'd just go away.

"Miss Bernadette!" His voice was a little louder.

She heard the jangle of keys. He was going to come in!

Heart pounding, Bernadette reached up with her right hand. The seal of blood that had dried her to the tub ripped along the arcs of her buttocks. She yanked the bath towel from the rack and threw it over her naked half. "Don't come in!" she cried. "I—I'm in the bath!"

The keys on the big ring that hung from his belt jangled and clunked against the front door.

"I'm not decent!" Bernadette shrieked.

"I'm sorry," Timo's voice was grim, although he genuinely sounded apologetic. "But I've got to inspect your apartment. There's a no pets policy. I can hear animal sounds through your floor."

Animal sounds! The young couple who lived in the apartment beside hers had sex every Saturday evening. And every time the man had an orgasm, he brayed like a donkey. Did Timo ever go check on them?

The door creaked open, and Timo's heavy boots thudded inside.

If they evicted her from the apartment, how would she find another place like this? So close to downtown and work. And almost afford-able. With a city vacancy rate below 1 percent! Rage surged through her veins, swelling, roaring through her body as if she were swamped by blood. Sweat poured from her. The droplets were tinged pink, beading her exposed skin.

Sudden silence rang in Bernadette's ears.

How loud the creatures had been. But now the noise was gone.

They knew ... the blood creatures knew. Having issued from her body, maybe they could feel her feelings. She squeezed tight her eyes and thought as loudly as she could. *Be still. Be silent. Danger!*

"It's nothing!" she said out loud, trying to sound cheerful. "I was watching an animal documentary. But now it's over."

"Sorry," Timo said. His heavy tread moved past the closed bathroom door and down the hallway toward the kitchen. "You don't have to come out. I'll just take a quick look a—"

*Thud. Thud. Clatter.* Things falling from a height. *Bang, bang, bang.* Like someone kicking the kitchen cupboards with a workboot.

Bernadette stared at the closed bathroom door.

Silence.

"Timo?" Her voice cracked. "Timo?" she said, a little louder.

He did not reply.

Bernadette's teeth began to chatter. She had to do something. She swaddled the heavy bath towel between her thighs, holding the ends in her right hand, from both the front and back sides of her body. She kept the tension taut against her crotch so that the material wouldn't slide downward and stepped out of the tub.

The heat bulb reeled above her head. So dizzy. How long had she lain there? When had she last eaten? She was so thirsty. So very hungry. She clutched the sink with her left hand, her faculties floating so high above her head she couldn't even turn on the tap. She leaned there for several long minutes.

The silence stretched like hours.

Hands patting against the walls, Bernadette tottered along the dark floorboards toward the kitchen.

A malformed moon shone through the window. It was still night. Or it was already tomorrow. The entire day spent bleeding creatures into the tub. Long shadows of the low light undulated across the floor. Glittered along the curved sides of overturned glass jars.

They'd eaten so much of him, so quickly.

*His bones. How will I get rid of them? Someone will see me. I'll be caught.*

The blood creatures squirmed and writhed along Timo's exposed bones. The clots did not eat each other. They had found something better. Then the sounds of crunching. Rasping. Like a school of beaked parrotfish eating coral. They were eating his bones for her.

"Thank you," Bernadette whispered. She pressed her fist against her lips.

Were the authorities ever to discover what happened, was she to blame? How could she be? She hadn't done it. The blood creatures had. Even if they were *of* her, they weren't really her ...

The sounds of crunching bones, slurping and sucking, made Bernadette's stomach rumble. Juices filled her mouth.

One of the creatures rose from the dark mound and sluffed toward her. Bernadette watched emotionlessly as it drew nearer. The size and shape of a fat, stumpy-limbed cat, it huffed through its too-small mouth. It humped its way to her side and bobbled upright to reach higher. It rubbed its head against Bernadette's open hand.

She was motionless. The curve of the blood cat's head was warm. It smelled sweet. Fresh. Alive.

Bernadette's fingers curled around the creature's head.

The creature crooned.

She looked down at the writhing mound of her blood born. They were eating everything. Sliding through the emptying sleeves of Timo's shirt, the legs of his work trousers with the movement of leeches. They even ate his hair. The little clots chewed each strand, like caterpillars munching grass. The largest clots, as big as half-grown puppies, tunnelled through the cloth, eating everything they could find. The sounds of chewing, crunching, cracking as loud as a feast of lobsters. Only his clothes would be left. His boots. Those she could wash in one of the shared washers, because it wouldn't matter if they found his DNA in it. He lived and washed his clothes there, too. Of course they'd find his DNA.

But of course.

If they asked to come inside her apartment … Bernadette froze.

Because maybe he'd left a note in his Day-timer to inspect her rooms. Maybe he'd told the building owner about his suspicions. When enough time had passed and no one had heard from Timo, they would come around looking. And then everything would fall apart.

"*Purrrrr*," the blood cat thrummed. It batted its head against her palm so she would continue to whisper her fingertips across the warm slick of its head.

Her mother was right, after all, Bernadette thought. She had to take care of her own business. Even if Timo's death wasn't something she'd wished or imagined, not something she'd physically hastened, blood was on her hands.

She didn't think she'd committed a crime or sin. She'd had no such intention. As far as she could make out, this incident was a kind of accident of nature.

She felt bad, but she didn't feel guilty.

She didn't wish to be prosecuted by the state for this incident. The details were too lurid, and the thought of being turned into a public spectacle made her want to slit her wrists. There would be no return to a private life after such a thing.

No. It was very clear what she needed to do.

Bernadette carefully lowered herself onto the towel that had dropped to the floor. She closed her eyes as dizziness pitched into her senses. Her body weaved with it, as if she were riding out waves at sea. When she was finally able to open her eyes, all of the blood clots had gathered around her. Their featureless faces, their too-small mouths, were a little like the beaks of octopi edged with tiny teeth …

Wonder filled her chest. The body was wise, she thought. You only had to listen to it. "You know what we need," she said. Growls rumbled in her belly, and she began to shiver.

The creatures drew nearer, pressing sticky against her naked thighs, crawling up her legs, their eagerness as great as her hunger.

The blood cat leapt to her chest. Bernadette caught its warm squishiness with both hands. More solid than Jell-O, but softer than the jelly cup sweets that had caused choking in young children. She could feel a faint pulse of blood coming from deep inside it, keeping time to the steady throb of her own heart.

How rich and sweet the blood cat smelled. She raised the creature to her chin and nestled it in the curve of her neck.

It thrummed with contentment.

Calling. She could feel the blood inside her calling. Bernadette bent her head low and bit into the giant clot of blood. It did not burst, nor stream liquid; a luscious chunk came off, filling the inside of her mouth, slick and satisfying. She chewed it slowly to savour the warm, coppery taste, the perfect texture. So delicious. She could have wept.

The blood cat didn't make a sound. It seemed to surge toward her mouth, as if answering the call with its own body. Bernadette bit and chewed, gulped and swallowed, the blood cat quickly consumed. The hunger in her belly roared.

"More!" she moaned.

The creatures surged around her, and she grabbed them, the little ones falling into the back of her mouth like raw oysters. *Plip, plop, plip*. She chewed once, then swallowed, so easy, so unfathomably tasty. She was so low in iron. She was starving for it. And now she was eating it back. Twofold, she realized.

*Well*, she thought, *if he hadn't entered my apartment without permission, he wouldn't have come to this end*. He had, in fact, been trespassing on private property. She didn't have animals in her apartment, anyway. They had only sounded like animals.

"Oh my god," Bernadette groaned. She reached out with both arms and swept more clots toward her chest, heaped in a writhing, shimmering mound. She lowered her face into them. They tickled her cheeks, her closed eyelids. She smiled. The hair on her neck, her spine, tingling electric.

She opened her mouth wide and bit down. She gulped and gulped like a starving sea turtle eating an entire ocean of jellyfish. The sweet and luscious blood filling her need, filling her want. Satiating.

▼ ▼

Bernadette roused from her state of deep relaxation. A golden light was shining through her window. The changeable moon had moved into the other hemisphere.

The kitchen was silent. A few spots of dried blood dotted the tiled floor. Timo's clothes were laid out, his shoes lying sideways at the bottom of his empty trousers. How neatly her creatures had eaten him. She couldn't see any blood on his clothing, and she was profoundly grateful. She folded up Timo's clothing and set his shoes atop the pile. She would take a bag of clothes to the Women's Hospital Auxiliary Thrift Store across town. No one would ever trace it back to her. They had a bin for off-hours drop-offs. His keys? She'd just drop them off one of the many bridges in the city. Maybe the Lions Gate. She could stop by and see the mute swans at Stanley Park on the way back.

She retrieved a large plastic bag from the pantry and filled it with her old cashmere sweater and a winter coat she hadn't worn for over three years. She placed Timo's clothes atop them, threw in several blouses she'd outgrown and three pairs of shoes she could no longer wear because the heels were too high, and added Timo's workboots. That ought to do it.

She set the bag beside her front door and then returned to the kitchen to spot clean the floor with a spray cleanser. After she was finished, the air smelled crisp. Like eucalyptus.

She filled the espresso pot with coffee and put it on the stove on high. She hadn't slept all night, but she felt so full of energy. So grounded and solid. She would run her errands after morning coffee, and maybe afterward, she'd go through her old books and CDs. Maybe it was time for a purge. To make room for new things. The coffee burbled, filling the small room with rich aroma.

She sat at the small kitchen table with her cup as the morning filled with the sound of city sparrows and starlings. The raucous laughter of seagulls who claimed building tops as islands for their nests.

Her cellphone rang.

Bernadette's eyebrows rose. Who on earth could it be? Her sister never phoned her. She retrieved the phone and glanced at the screen. It wasn't a number she recognized. She tilted her head to one side, then tapped the green icon. "Yes?"

"I'm really sorry," a male voice said. He was speaking so quickly and so breathily that it almost sounded obscene. "I'm really sorry to invade your privacy like this, I know you're not supposed to, but I was worried and I heard them talking and I wanted you to know."

"Slow down," Bernadette said crisply. "Speak clearly. Who is this?"

"I'm sorry," the voice said more slowly. "It's Mathew. From work."

Bernadette said nothing.

"I got your number from payroll. I'm sorry!" he entreated. "It's just—you've been gone for three days! Without calling in. The managers were getting mad. I heard them saying something about your Bradford score. And something about early retirement. I just wanted to warn you ..."

Bernadette took in the information. Three days. Well. After she dropped off the clothes, she ought to go to work, she thought.

"Thank you," she said, surprising herself. She actually felt grateful. To nervous Mathew. Who had no sense of privacy or decorum.

"I know that you don't like me!" he blurted. "Nobody likes me. I make people uncomfortable and I don't know why and I try to be friendly, but it never works." There was a ragged pause. Bernadette could picture him dragging his forearm across his eyes. "But I like you," Mathew whispered. "I want us to be friends."

Bernadette nodded. "I understand," she said. She took a sip of her coffee. "It's very brave of you to share your true feelings," she said. She meant it. She would have never done such a thing herself.

A small sob came through the cellphone. "Do you think so?" Mathew whispered.

"Thank you for sharing this information. It was thoughtful of you. I'll see you later today at work."

"Okay." Mathew sounded hopeful. "I hope you're feeling better!"

Bernadette smiled. A smile that filled her face with a golden light. "I feel good."

She placed her phone in her purse, the smile lingering in the corners of her lips. She ran her palms down the sides of her buttocks. Felt small flakes of dried blood. *I'll take a quick shower*, she thought.

As she adjusted the temperature of the spray and stepped into the tub, she watched the last bit of blood flow down the drain.

What would happen during her next cycle? She slowly turned, so that the hard needles of heated water pecked at her face, streamed down her body. Ohhhh, it felt so good.

She slicked her palms down her face, her chest, her breasts, and over her round belly.

Hot water seeped between her closed lips. She swallowed. Oh, remarkable life ... Every cell in her body sang.

# 75

**Justin Ducharme**

75 skin-covered robots tangle like webs inside my memory,
spinning souvenir networks of every daddy date turned
meal ticket, turned regular. Deep-pocketed men with an even deeper
sense of self-hate—I've assumed every position imaginable.
The monster in their closet. That boy who beat them up for looking.
The men who liked it and the ones who pretended they didn't.
Reminded that on our backs, boys like me can change your world.
Swallow it whole. Sweat ridden. A dark sparkler of your
repressed fantasies. The white man's up-and-coming on my
down-and-going. Small talk never was my strong suit.
I prefer to get deep. Because what the fuck's the point if you're not
cumming? Because the rent is due and the loneliest men pay it forward.
Because sometimes being the monster in their closet means you don't
have to be yours. Because 75 dates at two hundred dollars an hour
paid the rent. Because everybody wants to be somebody and if you don't
breathe in, a person can be anything for ten minutes.

# AN INVISIBLE MAN IS HUMPING A VAMPIRE
Steven Cordova

An invisible man is humping a vampire.
And since the invisible man has disclosed
to the vampire that he's positive, and the vampire
has likewise disclosed to the invisible man
he's positive, the vampire cries, "Oh yeah, baby,
come on, cum in me. Fill me up with those babies."

The invisible man and the vampire have a baby—
a precious vampire baby who becomes invisible
each night as it heads out to hunt, and who, late
one stormy night, heads out and never returns,
never comes crawling back to visibility
or its two AIDS-cocktail-guzzling daddies.

The invisible man is humping the vampire—
but in their minds they are out looking
for their invisible vampire baby, calling out
its name, wary that the longer they search
the more they'll be shunned, until, finally—
calling! calling! cumming!—the invisible man

and the vampire are forced to admit
even their own offspring fears them.

# THE MINOTAUR AND THESEUS (AND OTHER BULLSHIT)

Ben Rawluk

**1.**

There are Minotaurs everywhere. Each time he runs into one, he freezes and has to remind himself that they aren't real, that they're fans, people wearing costumes. They wear bull's heads made out of cardboard, chicken wire, papier mâché, and they keep stopping him. *You look so real*, they say, brushing their fingers along the fur line of his neck. He bristles, stopping a roar.

The party was his sister's idea. She says he needs to get out more, like he isn't a monster, isn't supposed to be dead. Then she disappears in the middle of the living room, leaving him with a bunch of loud, drunk people he doesn't know. He hovers in an overcrowded living room, uncertain where to sit or stand or *be*. He doesn't know where to look. He keeps thinking he sees Theseus, his stomach twisting each time. He does and doesn't want to run into him. He digs his fingers into the soft meat of his belly.

He hides in the bathroom until someone pounds on the door.

In the labyrinth, the Minotaur never knew what to do when they sent the human sacrifices in. Sometimes he'd sit in his bedroom and listen to bad grunge, or reread the same ten paperbacks, or do yoga. He couldn't go looking for them; if he did, he'd have to deal with the whole *eating people alive* thing. Like, people expected it of him, but it wasn't like he'd ever go through with it, and the conversation was always awkward. Sometimes people looked disappointed, and he couldn't deal with that.

**2.**

The Minotaur's sister is an angry drunk. She shows up at the convenience store on nights when he's working and stops him in the middle of restocking the shelves to berate him into taking a break with her, into giving her a strawberry slushie for free, into listening to her complain.

It's always about *that asshole. That asshole who seduced me, that asshole who left me waiting for him on the beach all night. That asshole* was on a talk show or a podcast or a magazine cover and now she's upset all over again. *I hear he's going to be on the new season of* The Argonauts. The Minotaur's sister chain-smokes while she complains, the pair of them hunched together on the curb out front.

*I just don't get why it doesn't bother you*, the Minotaur's sister says. *After what he did to you.*

The Minotaur doesn't want to talk about it. He stares at the cars roaring past. He drinks his slushie too fast, gives himself brain freeze to avoid answering the question.

**3.**

The first time he ever saw himself die, it was a cartoon. There were sound effects, like the plastic stretch of a neck right before the sword sliced through, the muddy galoshes squish of a bull's head slapping against stonework. He tries to draw a line from himself to the cartoon monster. He isn't a giant, doesn't devour virgins whole, and his head is still attached to his body.

He's got a big head, sure, but he's scrawny. He wears ratty old track suits out of his brother's closet. At work, he drags a mop and a yellow bucket filled with grey water up and down the aisles. After work he shuffles around his basement suite, from the futon to the kitchenette to the floor in front of the TV. He stands in the shower with his head at an angle to keep his horns from scraping the tile. In between, he walks around the neighbourhood, head down, trying not to think about the relentless emptiness of the sky.

**4.**

Hercules is playing beer pong in the basement. Biceps bulge underneath a pale-peach polo, a golden lion skin slung loosely over his shoulders. People cluster around the table, laughing and shouting, a drunken chorus. The Minotaur hovers at the bottom of the stairs, reminds himself that this isn't a deleted scene from *The Argonauts*.

If this were a deleted scene, this is how it would go: The Minotaur would claw his way out of the underworld to get revenge on Hercules. *You killed my father!* he'd roar. *You chased him through the woods and tore him apart.* There would be a flashback, Vaseline-smeared footage of the Cretan Bull as it ripped across the island, snorting and slobbering. Hercules and Theseus would team up to kill the Minotaur, once and for all.

This isn't a deleted scene, though. A Ping-Pong ball ricochets off a wall and slaps the Minotaur between the eyes. Everyone turns, giggling, everyone sees him. *Oh shit*, Hercules says. Hercules, who has killed so many monsters. Who can probably smell them. *My buddy Theseus should see you*, he says, like the Minotaur is performing a keg stand.

**5.**

When Birdbrain finally flew away, he didn't bother saying goodbye. He was only there in the first place because of his father. His father had built the labyrinth, and now they were locked inside. Birdbrain hung out with the Minotaur to avoid his father.

They'd hide in the Minotaur's bedroom and play video games for hours, Birdbrain squawking trash talk while Bellerophon slaughtered the Chimera on screen. They'd end up wrestling, flipping each other over on the ratty mattress, grunting and snorting like monsters, and then—well.

One day, Birdbrain's father built wings out of garbage, old sheets, paperback novels, and they flew away. The Minotaur should have seen it coming, probably. It wasn't like they'd ever used the word *boyfriend*. It wasn't like Birdbrain had ever wanted to talk about it at all.

The Minotaur wasn't pissed—not really, not for very long, not when he heard about what happened. Birdbrain had dropped like a stone into the sea. He drowned. The Minotaur lay on his stomach. The Chimera bashed Bellerophon's head in as tinny techno music played.

**6.**

There were nights when the Minotaur's stepfather came to visit. Visiting meant standing outside the Minotaur's bedroom and watching him silently, hands behind his back. The Minotaur's stepfather always brought security guards in cheap suits with him; they'd stand on either side of him, trying to stay still but constantly fidgeting. The Minotaur didn't know what his stepfather was there for, not really. Maybe he was waiting to see if the Minotaur was finally going to become a real monster.

There were nights when the Minotaur thought maybe they could find something in common, what with their fathers both having been bulls. There were nights when the Minotaur thought maybe his mother would finally visit, at least once.

After Theseus escaped, after he blew everything up, the Minotaur saw his stepfather one last time. He expected his stepfather to finish the job, expected *something*. He didn't. He said, *You're on your own now*, like all of this had been a favour, like the labyrinth was a kindness.

7.

Everybody knows the story of Theseus and the Minotaur. Theseus practically has it down to an anecdote, can recite the entire thing with a mic clipped to the lapel of his tailored purple suit. The noble Athenian youth, shining boy hero offered up as a sacrifice. The beautiful island princess sweet-talked into helping him escape. The terrible monster waiting at the heart of the labyrinth.

There's another version, one that the Minotaur tells himself: sprawling together on a bare mattress in the dark, being asked for the first time what he wanted, what he would do if he wasn't in the labyrinth.

Neither story is exactly true though, is it?

8.

It's not like he didn't look for other Minotaurs, other *real* Minotaurs. If he wasn't the only one then he couldn't just be some dickhead god's stand-up act about bull fucking. *I can't be alone*, he said, while customers stopped him in the middle of ringing up their late-night munchies to ask to take a selfie with him. *I can't be alone*, he said, but found no one exactly like him anywhere.

There were other monsters, at least. They were on apps, on message boards. There were zines, apparently. He made friends, found himself passing the hours behind the counter texting with them, but everybody was different. One friend, a Cyclops, came from an entire island of one-eyed giants. Closest he'd ever come to a hero was when his cousin was blinded by some asshole with a bow and arrow. *They're making it into a movie*, he said. The Minotaur stopped responding after a while.

There are others. The Gorgons don't post selfies. There are mornings when the Minotaur takes the long way home after work, drifting through a parking lot frequented by harpies. Their bodies are nebulous, feathery enigmas. Sometimes they shout abuse at construction workers, imitating their catcalls. He feels uncomfortable every time, doesn't know what keeps drawing him there. The harpies seem uninterested in being people, largely, and watch him when he passes like they can *smell* who he is.

### 9.

Whenever the Minotaur pictures running into Theseus again, he never imagines an audience. But when it does actually happen—when he escapes the party, stumbling into the backyard and freezing when he sees Theseus, *that asshole,* smoking a joint and dangling his bare feet in the swimming pool—it's like the Minotaur's the last person outside. Theseus is *surrounded* by people in Minotaur costumes, all of them trying to catch his attention, asking for autographs, begging him to tell them what it was like, what it was *really* like in the labyrinth, while the real Minotaur braces himself against white stucco and wishes the gods would save him. They do that, sometimes, rescue people from awkward situations by changing them into trees or echoes or constellations. But maybe they only rescue people-people, not monsters. Monsters are supposed to escape awkward situations by dying, after all.

Theseus is arranging the Minotaurs—the *fake* Minotaurs, heads like pinatas—into a line. It's well after midnight now, which means it's time for the Minotaurs to run. On nights when the Minotaur is at work, cosplayers often interrupt him, a roaring mass taking up the entire sidewalk and rushing in a given direction. Watching them always makes him feel even more alone.

Theseus slams a red Solo cup of cheap beer and burps. He's artfully dishevelled, as though he has a stylist on hand inside. He looks like he's in the middle of a music video, like maybe a singing career is what comes after a season on *The Argonauts.* When the Minotaur has pictured seeing him again, he's always imagined Theseus the way he was that night in the labyrinth—soft, sarcastic, the patchy beard, the anxiety sweats. He's pictured it a thousand ways: Theseus kissing him, fucking him, making awkward conversation, the gods transforming the Minotaur into a man, the gods transforming Theseus into another Minotaur, the two of them making their very own *Argonauts* porn parody, licking and sucking each other, their flesh melding together, becoming trees, becoming constellations, and Theseus finally, *finally* killing him. Now that Theseus is here, in front of him? The Minotaur is blank. *I waited for you* isn't good enough.

And Theseus doesn't even realize he's here.

The fake Minotaurs are stretching. The fake Minotaurs are drunkenly singing pop songs by Orpheus, by the Muses, by Apollo. Someone has handed Theseus a red flag, and all the Minotaur can think is *that asshole*. He could wait, stay behind, finally say something, but all he can think about is all of these jerks with their tinfoil horns, the red flag. He remembers standing in the open door leading out of the labyrinth, his stepfather watching him. He remembers Theseus—that *other* Theseus, the one from that night—asking him where he'd go.

# CRYPTID CRUISING

Avra Margariti

In St. James's Park a lilting voice speaks
Polari, a young cluster of men compare battle scars
and bullet shell necklaces by the lavender shrubs,
shirts hanging open, peeks of rough-terrain skin
under street- and moonlight.
Farther up the path, shrouded in moth-eaten darkness,
someone is laughing or sobbing.
Figures lean against scarlet oaks, eyes pinned ahead,
necks collared in colourful handkerchief code.
In the deepest part of the park, where even the police
daren't patrol the cruising spots, a giant
knocks against a wrought-iron lamppost.
Tattered wings aquiver, antennae erect as dancers,
Mothman seeks a surrogate moon
decades before the newspapers capture him
across the pond. I tap his shoulder and he turns
his trillion compound eyes on me.
I offer him a smile and a smoke,
watch his abdomen fluff out, fractal eyes
fixed not on the flame of my silver pocket lighter,
but upon my own form, as if for tonight
my bioluminescence is more than enough.

# INVERT

Saskia Nislow

she likes the backstroke best
and so the creature swimming beneath
falls in love with her backwards

imagining the gills she might have:
how they must open in the sunlight
aching for salt water

framing the shadow of her face
liver red
gaping

if it lay back
and let the current string its body
out like a weather vane
it could look just like her
if it weren't so afraid

it would wrap itself around
the warmth of her
and they could float together
pressing the surface from both sides

a scum line forming between them
which is
anyway
a slurry of sea and flesh

# STRANGE CASE

Eddy Boudel Tan

HENRY IS SMOKING A CIGARETTE, looking exactly as I imagine him when I masturbate. Neither tall nor especially muscular, yet possessing gentle curves and crevices I worship in secret. A swimmer's build, I suppose one might call it, though he's never before mentioned swimming. He stands in a corner of the parking lot while looking up at the gloomy sky, smoke drifting past his lips.

I come here when I want to be alone. My first instinct is to retreat, but he sees me before I can slip back through the door, his eyes squinting in my direction almost accusingly, as though he knows. But then his lips widen into a soft smile.

"Jack," he says, pointing upward. "Look."

A curtain closes over the sky, black and rippling. It takes a second for me to see the beating of individual wings. They move to a silent rhythm, powering the darkness east.

He turns to me. "Those crows travel across the city in the same cycle every day. Over thirty years, the same ritual."

"Huh." The silence that follows is unbearable. I sense myself about to say something pointless before the words even form. "Shouldn't you know better?" I glance at the cigarette between his fingers, trying to smile coolly so he knows I'm being playful, though I'm sure I look painfully awkward.

He shrugs. "On average, doctors smoke more than most professions. The stress."

"We're not doctors yet."

"I'm practising."

He smiles in the way I'd attempted, so comfortable in his skin despite the bleached white polo and khaki shorts. It's the same demeaning uniform worn by all the volunteers, but it clings to him while it hangs limply on me. We're different. He's sandy haired and knowingly beautiful. I'm the shy guy who's easily ignored. Not hideous by any means, but invisible.

Henry drops the remains of his cigarette, crushes it against the asphalt with his shoe. "See you inside," he says before pushing through the doors. I mumble a response, then wait a few minutes before following.

I can smell the sickness beneath the sanitizing chemicals. The halls of the care home are offensively bright, and the attempts at cheerfulness have the opposite effect on me—bees made of construction paper taped to the walls, group photos of the residents at a picnic. I smile at the nurses that pass, and it doesn't feel fake so much as automated.

I'm disgusted by sick people. I'd never say it aloud, but it's true. Skin that's sallow and damp, eyes discoloured and unlit from the inside. Their weakness clings to them like humidity, both desperate and docile, and I despise it.

You may question, then, my choice to study medicine, but you've never met my parents. I'd want to tell you I didn't have much say in the matter, that being the Lam family's first doctor was preordained, but I'd stop myself because of how silly it would sound and say instead that I just want to help people.

My classmates insist they enjoy their time volunteering here. They claim the residents are inspiring, though their explanations boil down to the simple fact of these people remaining alive for as long as they have. And so I'm forced to play along, pretending this place is something other than a reminder of what will become of us if we refuse to die.

Henry is a rare instance of beauty among the waste. He makes me believe we might always be young.

▼ ▼

My bedroom is dark apart from the bluish glow of the screen in my palm. I scroll through profiles of faces, abs, and other body parts. An endless carousel of loneliness. The men staring back at me blur into each other, becoming an amorphous reflection of what everyone thinks the other desires.

A man with thick hair and grey eyes stops me from scrolling. He's sitting with a black Lab cuddled in his lap, and they have matching smiles. The text states he's a web developer who grew up in a town called Port Hardy, and I almost make it to the end before one line stands out from the rest.

*Please be fit, masc, and not Asian.*

My jaw clenches, but then it melts into a smile. I decide to send him a message.

*Cute dog*

His response is immediate. The words send a ripple of warmth along my skin, and I already feel a connection with him.

*thanks ;)*
*doing anything fun tonight?*

> *Just got back from soccer*
> *So sweaty still*
> *I need a shower haha*

*i've got a shower you can use*
*;)*

He doesn't know I've never played soccer in my life. He doesn't realize I don't have the pale-bluish eyes or arrogant grin evident in my profile pic, a face so different from mine. This man wouldn't be interested in Jack Lam, crouched in the corner of a darkened room. This man wants Hayden, the pale eyes and grin he sees in the brightness of his screen. Hayden plays soccer. Hayden drinks whisky and dances shirtless at the bar. Hayden has eight inches and abs and everything else he knows they want.

Hayden is nothing like me, and yet more me than anyone knows. I'm free to say what I want and to take it.

The man asks to see how sweaty I am. Predictable. I search a folder filled with images of anonymous skin that are saved for moments like these. Each body is a little different in the shapes of their nipples and navels, but all of them are Hayden nonetheless. I choose one displaying a V of muscle that curves sharply toward grey sweatpants worn low on the waist.

*nice show me more*

*Not so fast*
*Your turn*

A few seconds pass before an image appears. The skin is waxen against the overexposed lighting, bringing to mind the poached chicken my mother used to make. Normally I'd still be aroused by the thickness of his arms and the veins that snake along his cock—he's laid down all his cards, no art of seduction here—but instead I'm sickened by the sight, an allergic reaction, almost. His body is young and objectively beautiful, but I see it aging before my eyes, deteriorating until it's nothing but sagging skin on bone, akin to the wasted souls that stalk the halls of the care home.

I close the image and glance at the man's profile pic instead, so wholesome and animal loving. That one line of text screams at me.

*Please be fit, masc, and not Asian.*

My eyes feel dry as my thumbs glide along the screen.

> *Wanna play a game?*

*... ok?*

> *I'm cold tonight*
> *1886 Barclay*
> *#101*
> *There's a key hidden in the bush*
> *North side*
> *I'll be in bed*
> *Come find me*

*coming*

Sex comes so easily these days for men like him. He wouldn't know what it's like to be disqualified before he's even tried. A few swipes on a screen, and he gets what he wants. It never used to be so simple. Even the beautiful ones had to wander down shrouded trails to find someone to touch.

I don't know anyone who lives at 1886 Barclay, and there's no key hidden in the bush. I simply want to give this man a reason to search.

The window closes and the carousel begins again, the man with the black Lab already forgotten. I view each athletic body and angular jaw as Hayden would—every one of them would be lucky to have a moment of my time, to be considered for my touch. I'm more attractive now, more interesting. I ignore their descriptions of what they don't want because I know they will want me.

A familiar face stares back at me unexpectedly, pulling me into reality. It's Henry, his lips curled into a mischievous smile. His hair is a mess like a windswept beach, not parted neatly on the side the way he wears it at the care home. His eyes squint as they peer at me—not accusingly, the way he looked at me earlier, but as though he has a secret to exchange.

My muscles tense as my thumb hovers above his unreachable face, but then a cool calmness washes over me, dulling the static that normally crackles beneath my skin. I'm Hayden now. Henry will want me.

*You need a haircut ;)*

I stare at the screen, waiting. His profile leaves much to the imagination. There's only one sentence in his description: *Looking for love in a hopeless place.* Username: *poisonedego*

Finally, he responds.

*And you need a better line ;)*

What do I say next? This isn't just a random guy, some throwaway face made of pixels. I see him every Tuesday and Thursday afternoon, masturbate to the thought of him every night. Jack wouldn't be permitted a glimpse behind his public facade, and he'd ruin it if it were offered. This is my chance.

*You're right*
*Let's start over*
*So ...*
*I know a great barber.*
*Interested?*
*;)*

▼ ▼

Thursday arrives. The front doors slide open, and I'm greeted by the familiar scent of impending death and present decay. It doesn't repel me the way it usually does, though. I've been eager to return to this place for the past two days. Residents and nurses smile at me, and I smile back as though I were Prince Charming at the ball.

My spirit wanes as the afternoon drags on. I've caught only flashes of Henry, turning corners or marching down corridors, always in motion. I'm unclear as to how differently I'll act, if at all. Everything and nothing has changed.

What I do know is I want him more than ever.

Partway through the day, the volunteers gather in the break room for an announcement. I see the sandy colour of Henry's hair in the far corner. I want to step closer to him, but my legs refuse. The program coordinator gains everyone's attention with her booming voice. She's overly bright, using far too many superlatives as she announces the volunteer of the month. "He must be the nicest guy on earth," she claims, convinced, "and he shows how much he cares every single day."

She's talking about me. I'm stiff and bewildered amid the polite applause. They don't realize the smiles and soft words are part of the performance, and I wonder if anyone sees what lies beneath. I'm both troubled and amused by how convincing I must be.

Near the end of my shift, I sneak out the doors of the east wing to my quiet corner of the parking lot. I shouldn't be surprised to see Henry standing there with a cigarette between his fingertips. He looks innocent, with his hair parted tidily on the side, unlike the mess I've viewed on screen.

I feel an urge to divert course, but I remind myself that I know him intimately now. I've seen what he hides beneath his tucked shirt and ironed shorts. I know what makes him come.

*Tell me I'm sick.* I hear his voice speak the words he sent to my screen the other night and I feel a little bolder.

"Hey."

He turns to me, and I want to tell him he's sick and do all the things we said we'd do to each other.

"Well, if it isn't the volunteer of the month," he says. His lips curl into a playful smile, though it's not quite as devilish as his profile pic.

*Tell me I'm a sinner. That I need to repent.*

I picture him as a bruised runaway, as I did the other night. A part of me is tempted to hit him across the face, to give him what he asked for, while the rest of me wants only to hold him in my arms, stroke his hair, and tell him it'll be okay. It's me, I want to tell him. Your Hayden.

Instead, I do nothing but shrug. "My parents would be so proud," I say, hoping he catches the sarcasm.

"I bet." He flashes me a smirk, and I'm relieved. "You know," he goes on, "it's true, what she said. You're nice. Nicest on earth might be a stretch, but very nice nonetheless."

I'm not sure what he's trying to do. It's a strange thing to say to someone he barely knows, and so I stand there in silence, unsure how to respond.

"Maybe I'm not, though."

"Come again?"

"Maybe I'm not as nice as you think."

He considers this for a moment, looking thoughtful, before stamping out his cigarette. "Maybe," he says as he heads for the doors.

▼ ▼

That night I lie in bed holding my phone above my face, silent and still. Forty minutes pass before Henry appears. My head feels a little dizzy at the sight of his tousled hair and narrow eyes. I resist the urge to reach out to him, but I don't need to resist for long.

*I hope you don't think I'm*
*a creep*

> *Why would I think that?*

*Because of what I made you*
*say last time*

> *No way*
> *It was hot*

*OK good, what a relief*
*I was worried*

*I worry, in general*

I imagine Henry lying on his bed, my words illuminating the contours of his face. He seemed so lonely the other night, so different from the version of him I'm permitted to see during the day. I wish he knew there's no need to hide from me.

> *You don't have to worry*
> *I get you*

*Thanks*
*But I doubt that*

> *Help me understand*

Why does intimacy come more easily when it's anonymous? Are we so far removed from our outward identities that it's painful to reconcile the two? Henry tells me things he claims he's never told anyone else, and I do the same. Despite progress and technology, we're all still wandering down shrouded trails to find someone to touch.

He tells me about his love for a childhood friend named Edward. They grew up together, swimming on the same team and attending church with their families.

They were the closest of friends, almost brothers, and they shared secrets with each other. At one point, Henry began to feel the pull we all know—lust and shame and confusion boiling beneath his stomach. He thought Edward must have felt it, too.

They were alone in Henry's room, empty beer bottles scattered around them. Edward was upset. He wanted to study art after they graduated that year, but his father didn't approve.

"You're the only one," he said to Henry. "Nobody else really knows me."

That was when Henry kissed him.

> *What did he do?*

*Pushed me away*
*Looked at me like I was a*
*stranger*
*I tried to calm him down*
*I just wanted to hold him*
*But he hit me, said I was sick*
*A sinner*
*I needed to repent*
*It angered me, so I hit him back*
*But he was bigger, and stronger*
*He hit me again*
*And again*
*I didn't want it to stop*

The words spill onto the screen, a splattered confession. I sense no reluctance. He might have held this within him for years, but now he's found someone to share it with, someone who cares. I'm unsure if I'm Jack or Hayden when I respond.

*He didn't deserve you*

*I liked it though*
*The pain*
*And I loved him, I think·*

*There's little difference between*
*love and madness*

The intimacy between us deepens in the days that follow. The world outside has been replaced by the screen in my hand, a window into something more meaningful. There are moments of lust. I tell him what he wants to hear, and I let him call me Edward. He sends me photos of his skin, and I can almost smell its purity. His face is never visible, but I feel so close to him still, as though I could reach out and make him shiver with my fingertips. We come together, and I imagine him on his bed with his stomach tensing and relaxing, wishing I were there to swallow the evidence.

Mostly, though, we talk about ourselves. I wait for him to mention med school or his shifts at the care home, but he never does. Instead, he explains to me why he's scared of being alone, and I admit I know exactly how he feels.

*But you're so beautiful,*
*Hayden*

*So are you*
*Nobody's immune to loneliness*

He's surprised to learn I'm still in the closet. I'm twenty-two and living with my parents, neither of whom truly knows me. I play the role of the son they've always wanted, yet they're not quite happy still.

It's not that I don't want them to know the truth. There's no other choice. My mother has been dying for years, so I can't give them another reason to worry. The transformation was slow as her body was seized by illness, and what's left barely resembles the woman I once knew. Hiding myself is the kindest thing I can do.

By the time the week comes to a close, Jack and Hayden have blurred into someone entirely new. I don't profess to play soccer or dance shirtless at the bar, but I also don't admit to Henry that I'm his classmate. The nice one. He continues to believe in my pale eyes and creamy skin, yet everything I tell him is true. I'm astonished by my own honesty. I'm neither Jack nor Hayden, or perhaps I'm both.

I fear that he'll suggest speaking over the phone or meeting in person. He never does.

The fluorescent lighting is stark and pervasive when I arrive for my shift on Tuesday. It's harder to smile back at the people I pass in the hall. My lips are strained as they pull upward, and it feels even less natural than usual.

My head is foggy from the past few days. I've let Henry peer beneath my cloak, and he didn't run. We've confided in each other what we've kept hidden from others—the things that shame us, scare us, ruin us with desire—but the closeness we've attained is marred by deception.

I'm not ready to see him in the flesh, the censored version of himself that he wears like a beautiful shell. I find myself wanting to reject this side of him.

My senses remain alert as I drift through corridors, but Henry is nowhere to be seen. Electricity sizzles along my skin and through my hair as the afternoon wears on.

I'm suddenly pulled toward the east wing by an inexplicable magnetism. My legs take me through the tunnel of bright lights and withering lives until I'm pushed out the doors and into the crisp, clean air.

"We've got to stop meeting like this." Henry is standing there, of course. Everything around us is grey apart from the orange end of his cigarette.

My first instinct is to laugh loudly, falsely, but I stop myself. Rather, I take a moment to breathe and readjust to the physical shape of him.

"We might have different methods, but we've got something in common," I say. "We come here to escape the suffocation inside."

He squints at me while he takes an unhurried drag of his cigarette, then smiles a little wickedly. "Maybe you were right," he says. "Maybe you're not as nice as everyone thinks."

"I tried telling you so."

Henry remains cool and calm. I search for evidence of the person I know him to be, for flashes of truth beneath his costume. I no longer care for this act or the role he plays. I crave the vulnerability, the perversion. I want to see the ugliness, the inward part of him disfigured by trauma.

But he doesn't allow it. He's become too good, too convincing. There are no cracks in his exterior. I see no turmoil or uncertainty. Nothing but cold, hard dispassion.

He studies me a little longer, then says, "Want to see something that'll break your heart?"

He leads me around the corner to a cluster of trees along the edge of a field. The sky stretches monochromatically overhead like a sheet of steel. He stops at a clearing in the trees and waits for me to see it.

Nestled in the grass are the bodies of two crows. Their feathers are unnaturally black against the muted backdrop. One's wings and talons are bent at crooked angles, while the other is huddled into itself.

"They must have belonged to the flock that travels east this time of day," Henry says, his tone sombre. "They're proud creatures. I bet they got into a fight."

Before I realize what's happening, I have him pressed against the trunk of a tree. His shirt is clenched in my hands, my claws, and my breathing is heavy and ragged. I see in his eyes that he's stunned. We stand there, clutching each other, while I inhale his scent of smoke and skin. Then my mouth meets his, and I taste the ash on his lips. He stiffens at first before his face leans into mine. His hunger reveals itself as he slides his hands beneath my shirt.

I've been wanting this for so long, and perhaps he's wanted it, too. I won't make him choose between Jack and Hayden. He can have it all.

"You make me sick," I say, my voice low. He pulls away from me slightly, squinting as he processes my words. I want him to know. I'm tired of pretending, utterly exhausted by it. I want him to know he doesn't have to pretend, either.

"What—"

I push against him harder and grip his neck with my hand, how I know he likes it.

"Jack, you're—"

"Shut your mouth, sinner." It feels different spoken aloud. It's a voice I've never heard before, a pitch and timbre I didn't know I possessed, but I keep to the script. "You're a filthy, worthless pervert. Repent for your sins."

There's only confusion in his eyes, then a flash of fear. His hands reach out to push me away, but I won't let go. My grip tightens around his neck as I pull myself closer. His elbow jabs me in the stomach, and he wrenches himself away. I have no control of my body as it lunges at him, tackling him to the ground. We roll across the grass until I have him pinned with my hands on his wrists, my legs around his groin.

"Get the fuck off me!"

"Shhh," I say. "It's okay. It's me. Hayden."

His face is twisted as he glares at me, helpless. There's a warm satisfaction in drawing the ugliness from such beauty.

"Who?" he stammers.

"You can call me Edward if you want."

His struggling stops. I search his eyes while he searches mine, and still I see no glint of recognition.

"I know all about you," I say, trying to soothe him with my quiet voice. "I'm sorry for tricking you with someone else's photo, but it's me. I'm Hayden."

He's still for a moment longer, squinting even more intensely, before he tries to wrestle free.

"What the fuck are you talking about?" he screams. "Get off me right now."

I feel the urge to hit him. That's what he wants, isn't it? He likes the pain. He said it himself. This is all part of the fantasy.

I look down on his frightened face, and my body shakes when I realize that I've also been deceived. This isn't the Henry I've come to know. I can see it in his eyes, no glimmer of understanding beneath the fear and confusion. His denial isn't just an act. He's never met Hayden, and he's not the person I've shared secrets with in the privacy of our screens. That other person could have hidden behind anyone's face and name, but he chose Henry's.

I can't stop my trembling fingers as they release his wrists and close around his neck. Henry's innocent—he was nothing but a mask—yet I still want to hurt him.

His eyes widen, white with panic, before he punches me in the gut. My balance falters, and his hands pummel me until he's free. He climbs to his feet and kicks me in the ribs. I double over, my vision blurring until he's a ghost.

"Fucking psycho," he says. I hear his feet take small, cautious steps away from me before they pick up speed, making soft sounds against the grass.

I lie on the ground with my limbs spread out, listening to the heaviness of my breath. I'm so tired, so incredibly tired. There's no point in moving or running after him. The greyness above is absolute, mirroring this physical world that's both blank and obscuring. I see nothing but the distorted look on Henry's face, wondering how I could have been so easily fooled. I should have known how deceptive a face can be.

All we want is someone to touch, don't we? Someone as defective as ourselves. I suppose I've followed the wrong shrouded trail, but there might still be something real at the end. I reach into my pocket and hold the screen above me. Let's find out who's on the other side.

# NAGA MARK RUFFALO DREAM

**beni xiao**

last spring i dreamt that i was walking through a forest
before being knocked out by a naga lady

and regaining consciousness (in the dream not irl)
in the Secret Naga Lair, where i'm presented
as an intruder to the King of Nagas.
it's mark ruffalo,

shirtless, with a long, shiny,
dark-grey snake tail. dream me is thinking,
*damn, naga mark ruffalo is kind of sexy lol* and

naga mark ruffalo says to me
"who sent you, and how did you find us here?"
and i'm like, "huh? i was just

walking through the forest and
your friend knocked me out and brought me here?"
naga mark ruffalo is like

"a LIKELY story!" and starts
wrapping his sexy naga tail around my body
to try and threaten me into telling the truth, except

a) i was already telling the truth, and
b) this is actually not scary, but rather uhhhhhh
#Arousing???

so dream me is like "please
sir, i'm not lying." i think he
misreads my embarrassed arousal for

fear. so he wraps himself tighter
around me, grabs my face
and sneers at me to

"tell the truth." i look him dead in the eyes
and say, "i am" but it comes out as sort of a moan???
i blush with mortification
and think that's when he realizes

i'm not scared, but turned on, and also
that i'm telling the truth. he too looks
mortified, and loosens his grip on me. just then,

i wake up. suddenly, i'm real me,
blinking at sunlight, just as bewildered
and embarrassingly aroused by
naga mark ruffalo as

dream me was. i keep hoping i'll
find my way back to his lair in my dreams,
while avoiding mark ruffalo movies irl.

# IN OUR OWN IMAGE

Matthew J. Trafford

"LET'S MAKE A BABY," he'd say sometimes. I'd had lovers say this before, in that callous way tops can have about them: *We haven't been using condoms but we just can't seem to conceive. I've been going in bareback but it's just not working.* We both used condoms, though; we found it more sanitary. I took this phrase to be a little quirk at that time in our relationship when the idiosyncrasies and small flaws were what began to bind us together.

"Let's make a baby, Marcus." I never took him seriously, because I never knew how serious he was about *me*—how could a connection this strong last for very long? That wasn't the way it happened, not for me or for anyone I knew. But when he cried in front of me for the first time, cried *sober*, cried and said he didn't want to be alone, that he was terrified sometimes that I would leave him, then I finally believed he was mine, and I began to think that maybe he was serious about a child.

Even though this potential child was safely in the future—we didn't even live together—I found out what the paperwork looked like, what we had to prove, whether an insurance underwriter and an actor-slash-sommelier could really afford a baby, and so on. When I mentioned this to him, he reacted badly.

"I don't want to adopt," he spat. "I want us to make one, you and me—a baby that comes from us."

I didn't know what to say, what he meant—what the hell was he talking about? But he seemed so sincere, so defenceless as he said it.

Soon after, he asked to move in, and I was ecstatic—finally my life might be as I had imagined. He would barely make an impact on my carefully decorated condo. I'd been to his place, of course, and he had very few belongings beyond his clothes, like some travelling magician or gap-year backpacker. So when he suggested he wanted the spare room, which I barely used, for his study, I figured that was an acceptable compromise. Men and their man caves. It was just an empty little room—an electrical outlet, a sturdy table, and a bench. Maybe he had a hunting rifle from his grandfather he would want to polish from time to time. Maybe he had some hobby that he engaged in once in a while when his life seemed too monotonous or his job too boring. Maybe he wanted to lay down old world reds and liberate them with flare at the dinner parties we would throw together. I could deal with these things. I had read about Bluebeard and his wives, the dangers of curiosity. And so I left him his one little room, the only place I didn't fuss over and clean and have complete anal-retentive control over.

When he did bring in his meagre baggage on the first of the month, there were no surprises. He had his tennis racket and his workout gear, an inflatable armchair—which I sternly forbade—a lamp, a guitar, some knick-knacks—among them, two polished onyx orbs he jokingly called his "balls"—and an urn that contained the ashes of his beloved childhood dog, Stanley.

We didn't have pets in my house growing up, though I often felt my brothers and sisters were acceptable substitutes. There was this old lady who lived across the street. I thought of her as very old, though probably she wasn't much more than fifty, which doesn't seem so far away to me now. Her husband was seventeen years older, and he'd had a stroke that left his face paralyzed and drooping like melting wax. She parked him on the porch, and he sat there in the shade most of the day. She'd feed him his lunch of baby food, not much different from what my younger siblings ate, and he'd drink through a straw, and he would groan at you with a little spasm of his right arm, which my mother told me was meant to be a wave and should be properly answered with a wave in kind and a greeting of, "Hello, Mr. Monahan." I complied with all my mother's instructions at that age, but I always felt a shudder of horror when he jerked at me and moaned. I always tried to cross the street so I could reasonably pretend to be out of earshot when I passed by.

The Monahans also had a dog, which my father called a Dogue de Bordeaux and my mother called a mastiff, who was very old and had severe hip dysplasia—I can say that now, though at the time I thought it was the result of an accident. Maybe the Monahans had dropped him out a window, for that was how he looked: all splayed out. Mrs. Monahan had rigged up a sling for him of her own design. You see these now with wheels attached, but hers was much more low tech, simply a swath of canvas that scooped up his hind legs, and she would walk him twice every day. If I ever saw her coming home from one of these walks, she would be red faced and puffing, sweating profusely, and as she rounded the corner Mr. Monahan would moan and wave, and the dog would howl, and altogether it was the most embarrassing scene I could imagine. I remember asking my mother why she did it—why she kept Mr. Monahan at home, why she didn't put the dog down. My mother had said, "She loves them." Something about the way she said it was so final and so commanding that I didn't ask her anything else. But I thought maybe my mother was a fool.

Things started going wrong on a Sunday, though I didn't know it then. On Sundays, we slept in, made greasy breakfasts to combat our hangovers, and spent the day being domestic and lazy and stupid. He'd read the paper for hours—dozing half the time—and I couldn't even manage to resent him for it because he looked so happy and so much like my father and because he was so unequivocally mine. So I would clean and do the laundry and hate it and love it at the exact same time.

On this particular Sunday I was going through the pockets of his jeans to make sure they were empty before throwing them in the washing machine, and I found a receipt from when we'd gone out for Chinese food a couple nights before. I crumpled it and went to throw it in the garbage, but suddenly he caught my arm in that rigid grip of his.

"I want that," he said. His eyes were on fire. I had thought he was sleeping, unaware of where I was or what I was doing.

"Okay," I said. I felt awkward. "Sorry. For taxes?"

"For our baby," he said. "This is part of who we are."

I kissed him dismissively, because I didn't know what else to do, and went back to sorting laundry. He put the receipt in the pocket of the pants he was wearing, but I wondered where it would end up. Was he making a scrapbook? Would I just be taking it out of another pair of jeans a week later?

There was a thing we liked to do sometimes when my mother would phone. She always picked the worst times, and no matter how innocently the conversation started, I inevitably ended up in tears, feeling criticized and small. He would start kissing my neck while I was still on the phone with her, and he'd slowly undress me as I made my excuses and tried to end the call, which always seemed to take forever. In the end he'd take my underwear off with his teeth just as I was hanging up and we'd go at it like teenage boys. I loved him for it. But a few times—this was after that Sunday with the receipts—I couldn't find my underwear afterward. I assumed they'd been kicked somewhere in the heat of things, but it bothered me not to be able to locate them. He didn't take it seriously and told me to lighten up. I was convinced we would have company over sometime and someone's dog or curious toddler would pull my skivvies out from under a couch, and we would all die of embarrassment. Eventually I gave up looking. It never occurred to me that he was taking them.

I can't explain how it felt when I found it. I think there's always some relief in that kind of a moment: this is it, this is the secret, this is the thing that's wrong with him that allows him to love me, this is what he was hiding, this explains every time I didn't feel totally happy even though I had this man to love me. It doesn't matter what you find—proof of another lover, a secret stash of porn, macabre pictures, strange costumes—once you've found it, something drops into place, a thousand tiny mysteries get solved, even as your stomach sinks below your knees and the room begins to spin.

We had tickets to see *Pygmalion* at the Grand, and I couldn't find him. One of my greatest pleasures was seeing him dressed up in formal clothes, sitting beside him in the dark and hearing his confident, booming laugh, feeling his hand on my knee. We were late. We couldn't miss it. And so I popped my head into his special room, a door I had never opened since he'd moved in, and I saw it, lying there on the table, about a foot and a half long, staring blankly up at me with the black globes he'd used as eyes. The head looked so large for a baby, the face a bizarre amalgam of the two of us—how did he make it so accurate? The bridge of his nose, the ridge of my brow. For a moment I just marvelled at how good a sculptor he was. I'd had no idea he was capable of something like this.

Its feet were pointing toward me, and I could see inside its body. He'd formed the frame from coat hangers, those ones from the dry cleaner's he told me he'd taken back, instead put to this other purpose, like my underwear, like so many lost and forgotten things. The body was stuffed with used condoms, tangled and stuck together like shed snakeskins, hardened with time and whatever we'd left in them. A baby of latex and soiled white cotton. There was hair in there, too, I could see it, though my eyes were not so good in the dim room that I could tell which one of us it had come from. My God, had he gone through the garbage digging for this stuff? Had he scraped hairs off the scummy shower soap and wiped them off his fingers into the innards of this disgusting thing?

A hot roil started inside my belly, and a copper taste filled my mouth as I realized the man I loved was so profoundly and completely insane that it was wrong for me not to have noticed. Criminal. Impossible.

And so, there was a choice lying there before me. I could reject the man who cooked for me and warmed my bed at night and snored softly beside me and killed spiders in the sink when I was too scared. I could denounce the man I loved for the lunatic he was, have him committed somewhere, treated, endure the sympathetic stares of friends as we all hoped he would get better, pretended things could still work out, even though we all knew they wouldn't. Or, I could lie to him, pretend not to have discovered this until he forced me to look at it.

And then he stepped out from behind me. He was staring at me, but he looked wrong; he was holding his jaw in a strange position that changed the shape of his face. I realized he was chewing something, his cheeks bulging with the mass of it. Our eyes were locked—I couldn't look away. I'd never seen the expression on his face before. He held his upturned palm in front of his mouth and carefully spat something white and pulpy into his hand. Then, finally, he looked away from me to the thing that he'd made and started stroking it, adding chubbiness to its left arm. This was where the receipts had gone, the newspapers that had never made their way to the recycling bin, the grocery lists and the Post-its I'd left to tell him that I loved him, the bits of paper that made up our ordinary lives, chewed and masticated into something he could mould, a saliva-soaked sludge he had pressed as a plaster with his fingers, shaping this thing before me.

I couldn't move. I knew that he would say something eventually. He had to. And I knew that, by what he said, my decision would be made.

"What do you want to call him?" His voice was hushed. It was the gentlest tone he'd ever used with me, and the most terrifying thing he had ever said.

I closed the door and left him to his final ministrations. I knew I should have done something responsible—called his family, maybe, to see if there was a history of mental illness I didn't know about. If maybe he had had this kind of episode before. That thought comforted me, somehow. Maybe as a teenager his parents had caught him creating a bizarre sex doll, maybe he had spent time at a facility that would take him back now and know exactly how to deal with this problem. And then he would return to me, whole again, and we would go on as if this had never happened.

But I knew there was no facility. And I was too scared to call his parents. I'd only met them a handful of times, at big family functions, and we weren't close. I didn't want to upset them, prompt them to come here, do something that could worsen the entire situation. I didn't know if I could make myself say the words to them.

And so I left. I went to Justin's house—we'd slept together once, but that was years ago. I'd always had the sense he wanted to start things up again, but I wasn't interested. I suppose that made us friends. What passes for friends. Anyway, I went there, and I asked for a drink.

"Do you remember ..." I trailed off. He arched his eyebrow at me as he poured honey-coloured whiskey into a cut crystal glass, curious and inviting. "Did I ever tell you about those neighbours I used to have as a kid?"

"Yeah, the really devoted wife? I think about her all the time." He handed me my bourbon, I changed the subject, and we drank. I don't even know how much we drank; I only remember the first four. I woke up on his couch with a terrible headache at 3 a.m., and I left without saying goodbye.

Then I walked all the way home, watching the neon lights give way to the daylight. I was prepared to do something. Grab some clothes, tell him I needed a little solo trip to adjust to my new life as a father— after all, I hadn't had as long as him to get used to the idea. Something like that, just to get me out of the house. It was reasonable. Or maybe

I could grab some things and sneak out before he even woke up. It was just before six. But when I got inside, all those thoughts disappeared.

I'll never know how he did it. I missed those first moments because of my night out, and now it was a secret thing between them how he'd made his hideous creation come to life.

At first I thought he was puppeteering—I actually reached out my hand and moved it over and below to see if there were any wires. Then I thought it must be animatronic, that there were motors inside, little tiny ones that made it move in set ways. I knew he'd spent some time in California right after college, and he never talked much about what he'd done there. Maybe he'd worked in movies, learned props and special effects before moving on to the secrets of the vineyard and coming back home.

But there was something so organic about it, the way its eyes actually found my face, they way they followed me when I moved around the room. It was paper white, vampiric, faint little lines of text like veins beneath the surface of its skin. And the eyes were black, so deeply black. They were stone; they were night.

That was when he asked me, "Do you want to hold him?"

For a moment I imagined myself as some modern-day Medea— I would dash its head against our Italian marble countertop. I would draw a warm bath and gently immerse it, not holding it down to thrash and drown, but letting it slowly dissolve, teasing it tenderly apart until it was only wire and floating latex refuse and mush in our tub. I would set it on fire and launch it off the balcony and let out a scream of victory, knowing all I had done was merciful, ultimately humane.

Then he handed it to me with a pleading, proud look on his face, a kind of smile I'd never seen. It was not warm when I took it. It felt cold and clammy against my arm, a dead fish. My flesh prickled. Instead of cooing or gurgling, it let out a pained, haunted moan. Or else I did. At any rate, I recognized the sound.

Then I said, "Hello."

# DAD MOVIE

## Kayla Czaga

In the movie, a secret agent and a marine biologist
must pair up to save the world from a sea monster

that the villains have engineered into an organic weapon.
The villains might be Russians, anarchists, neo-Nazis,

or terrorists. The movie doesn't linger on their identity,
insisting evil is eternal and interchangeable. My father

pours an Old Style Pilsner into his beer mug, as I pull
a Calgary Flames afghan across my lap

and crinkle open a bag of Old Dutch Salt & Vinegar.
We've seen this one before. The marine biologist

and secret agent don't want to work together.
He's hotheaded; she's a snob. Both of them revisit

their backstories as if dredging up rusty old crab traps.
If the movie was directed by Michael Bay, her button-up

will come undone beyond our suspension of disbelief
and the hero will ripple under his trench coat,

his bicep dwarfing her torso, echoing the sea monster.
My father clicks the volume up to cover my mother's

coughing upstairs. In this version, he and I are
sea monsters, lurking below. His afghan is patterned

with wolves and mountain ranges. If the movie
was directed by Clint Eastwood, the secret agent

has a lost daughter who will surface like flotsam
halfway through the plot. The marine biologist won't

understand their filial banter, recoiling into herself
like a hermit crab. The sea monster also has a daughter who—

with biological urgency—will carry out her father's work
once our heroes have blown him up. She will be much

harder to kill. Her eggs will be lethal and legion.
Sound pushes through our floorboards: the dishwasher

being emptied and reloaded, plates clattering
into cupboards. When I leave for the bathroom, my father

presses pause, pours another Pilsner, and relaxes into
the brown floral sofa that pretty much sums up my childhood.

If this were a Scorsese movie, there'd be no marine biologist,
no women at all, no monster except the one that slithers

inside each man, as my father drives home at dawn
from the aluminum smelter with the other

busted-up family men. All of this happened a long time ago.
Cigarette smoke curled above his head like tentacles.

His beer mug had a wooden handle and little flowers
etched into its amber body. If his life was a movie,

the mug would mean something, Wes Anderson–kitschy,
but we donated it to a thrift store in Parksville.

Once the movie ended, I would touch the few artifacts
on my father's shelves and think, *staging*, and wonder

what the ammolite shell, the hula girl bust, or the medical
compendium revealed about his character. Like a couple

of engineered plants that grow best in blue light,
we repeated this ritual most weekends. A close-up

of the ocean. Pan out to a treeline, research station,
two kids in the sand constructing a palace with a bucket.

Something disturbs the water's surface. Cut to:
the marine biologist lifting a vial filled with dark liquid.

The secret agent asks, "So, that'll kill it?" "It'll draw
the evil out of it," she responds. A green telephone rings.

Upstairs, my mother would be watching HGTV—
home improvement shows in a home that would never

improve, but settle into its rot like a shipwreck.
Its roof and windows weathered water

as best it could, given the conditions. The conditions:
the marine biologist looks up from her paperwork

to see the secret agent helping an old lady into a car
and immediately falls in love. But the secret agent

has been in love with her since the movie started
forty-seven minutes ago, having kept his feelings

sheathed in one-liners and macho responsibility.
With renewed energy and a rosy forehead,

the marine biologist finishes her work. Of course
my mother would be the marine biologist, studying us

under her microscope with scientific remove.
In the movie, my father punches a wall because

he loves her, dammit, and his emotional expression
is limited by Hollywood gender roles and early 2000s

special effects. A speedboat explodes. A seaplane
explodes. A submarine explodes. And I, their sea

monster, evil and beloved, wave one loopy tentacle
before my great eye goes glassy. During the credits,

my father would ask how school was going
and try to indoctrinate me on politics. Sometimes

he'd show me a photo album from his own youth,
which contained no movies, only staticky farmland.

Or he'd say nothing, just shuffle to the television
and open up the DVD player to put in the sequel.

# GHOSTS OF PRIDE PAST

Cicely Belle Blain

**"ARE YOU FUCKING KIDDING ME?"** Bradley says, looking at the splash of white cum decorating his newly polished badge on the nightstand. "Get the fuck out!"

Alex—although Bradley does not remember that that is his name—does not need to be told twice. He grabs the cash from the nightstand and legs it out the door.

Bradley heaves his body off the bed. "Fuck," he shouts gruffly, as the last of his father's 1940s cut-glass crystal tumblers falls and smashes at his feet. He grabs a lumpy, yellowing pillow and wipes the blood from his gnarled big toe before tossing it on the laundry pile at the end of the bed. *Tomorrow, I'll get to feel Derick's throbbing cock inside me,* he thinks to himself, and the thought puts his mind at ease.

He throws his arms out in a full body stretch and winces as his joints crack in defiance. Catching a glimpse of himself in the bedroom mirror, he meets the sunken, bloodshot eyes of a self he does not recognize. He sucks in his low-hanging gut, lamenting the version of himself that exists only in his mind: tanned, muscular, glistening with youth.

He presses his cheeks hard, as if to push the wrinkles back in time, letting out a rough grunt when he is unsuccessful.

Bradley slides the screen door open and steps onto the balcony. He drags on a cigarette, tapping red-orange embers off the side, watching them disappear into the night. A thunderstorm throws Vancouver into an ugly chiaroscuro. Ten floors below, the tendrils of Davie Street slope down on one side toward the ocean. He waits for the head rush, desperate to feel something as he looks down at the neighbourhood he once loved.

"I can't stand what this place has become," he says to the night and the smell of piss.

He misses fucking twinks in alleyways and trading blow jobs for anything that made him forget. He misses the 2 a.m.'s when the West End felt like the Wild West. He throws his cigarette butt over the railing and heads back inside for a glass of Jack before he can allow himself to think the thought he knows is true. *I can't stand what I have become.*

Bradley unlocks his phone with his thumbprint, pauses to admire the rim job he's giving Derick in the video still open on the screen, and asks Siri to open UberEats. As he presses *place order* on two stuffed-crust pepperoni pizzas with extra cheese, a frantic knock vibrates the damp frame around the front door.

"Fuck off!" he shouts, but when the visitor knocks three more times, he heads to the door. Sighing, he laments the peephole replaced by a wad of spackle ever since he cracked the glass slamming the door on some seventeen-year-old who'd been convinced he was a top. He pulls the door open, the chain catching it like a leashed Rottweiler.

"Yes?" he says gruffly, letting the disturber see only half his face and one thick bicep.

"Mr. Scranton, please let me in!" a skinny teenage boy begs, peering up at him.

Bradley considers the boy, trying to place him in one of the other apartments on the fifteenth floor. *How does he know my name?* Bradley asks himself. *Is he from number 6, the single mother with three kids and three baby daddies? Or number 11, the oversized family from someplace in Africa?*

"What do you—" Bradley begins, but the boy is small enough to slip under the chain, past him and into the living room.

"Hear me out!" the boy says, out of breath and trembling. "Please, sir, I came to warn you."

Bradley pauses, searching for the right response, wanting to be aloof and assertive at the same time. The right answer comes to him immediately, and he reaches for his gun in the holster hanging from the coat hook. "Why the fuck are you in my house, kid?" he asks, fighting the tremble in his throat and looking down at the boy, who is now on his knees with his arms raised.

"Don't shoot! P-please, s-sir. It's me, Jayden Marlborough, from number 6."

"Marlborough?" Bradley glances at the blinking ankle monitor poking out above the boy's knock-off Jordans, a wry smirk forming. He slightly lowers the department-issued Smith & Wesson, its muzzle still facing Jayden. *I wasn't going to use it, of course*, he tells himself, but thinks up a quick list of self-defence excuses anyway.

"Sir?" Jayden asks, bringing Bradley out of his thoughts. "I don't want to alarm you, but I had to warn you, man—I mean sir. They are coming."

Bradley opens his mouth to ask *who* or to tell the kid to fuck off, but his jaw locks in a feeling of horror that no tough-guy facade could overcome. The boy is standing and twice the size now than he was before. His eyes turn from bloodshot to a deep crimson, his skin no longer burnt umber, but pumice grey.

Bradley's military reflexes kick in, and the semi-automatic is back in line with Jayden's chest. Without hesitation, he gives the trigger a soft pulse, like switching on the coffee pot in the station break room. The bullet flies through the boy's torso, shatters a few vinyl records, and lodges itself in the opposite wall. But the boy is still growing, rising and moving toward Bradley, his translucent body unharmed by the bullet. Bradley empties the magazine, only smashing more of the ornaments inherited from his bitter mother.

He is backed up against the front door and has no option but to cower into the corner, raising his hands above his head. "Please ..." he whispers.

Jayden's ghoulish figure hovers above him, cocking his head from side to side as if to take in the pathetic form of Bradley. He retreats momentarily, only to rush at full speed at Bradley, who lets out a squeal and clenches his eyes shut. Almost unrecognizable now, once-Jayden flies through Bradley and the closed door, vanishing. There is a sudden, eerie quiet except for the low hum of the ankle monitor lying on the wooden floor.

"That fucking twink spiked my whisky," Bradley says out loud in the empty apartment. "Or maybe it was that line last night at Junction? Or ..." he scours his fragmented memories of the last week for any explanation of the past five minutes, concludes that the confiscated supply in the back of his Dodge Charger is not to be fucked with anymore, and pulls himself off the floor, feeling every bit his early sixties in his bones.

"Did you shit yourself, Bradley?" a voice from nowhere forces another involuntary squeal from Bradley.

"Who the fuck are you?" he shouts, trying to sound gruff and menacing, but coming off more like a middle-school bully. "What do you want from me?"

"Sit down and let's talk," the voice says. It's soft, almost kind.

Bradley takes several firm steps toward the living room. *Don't be a pussy.* In the doorway, he stops, more confused than scared.

The living room is empty, but the television is crackling with white noise. He lets his heartbeat slow, reminding himself that he is the proud owner of probably the oldest television set in Vancouver. He laughs, thinking of Derick's suggestion to get a smart TV so he can "cast" his phone to the big screen. The TV hisses and fizzes louder, the picture wavering between grey streaks and CBC News.

"How could I ever replace you?" Bradley says to the TV. "Big behind, big knob—just my type." He cringes at the shakiness in his voice.

Suddenly, the grey fuzz disappears, replaced by a head and shoulders against a black background. It's a beautiful, godlike face—not chiselled and masculine like Derick's, not a face he wants to finish all over, but a face he wants to paint or carve in marble.

"Still scared?" the figure asks. Bradley trips on a shard of vinyl and tumbles backwards onto the couch. In seconds, he is up again, feigning fearlessness.

The figure transcends the television screen, becoming three-dimensional before Bradley's eyes. It is tall and translucent, pumice grey like the once-Jayden, but with a shimmering pink-orange aura. Bradley follows the delicate cloud being as it glides the eight feet across the living room and into the kitchen. He walks through the cool, glittery mist left in its wake.

"Take a seat, Brad."

"I'll stand, thanks. And don't touch anything."

The figure has a humanoid body, though the fridge is visible through its soft, rolling midsection. Bradley is overcome by the scent of bergamot, rose petals, and ocean breeze—a far cry from his apartment's usual odour of sex and whisky. *Who is she?* he thinks, mouth open in a circle.

"I don't find archaic binary pronouns particularly becoming of ... all this," the figure says, gesturing up and down their body, "and no, I can't read your mind, just your face. Look, I don't have much time."

The figure glides across the room, not bothering to skirt the kitchen island as they phase right through its corner. Seeing them up close, Bradley admires their heart-shaped face, warm brown under the greyish veneer, more shocked at his ability to appreciate their beauty than at the presence of a ghost in his kitchen. They reach out a hand to his, and Bradley is surprised to feel the cool, soft palm in his own.

"Hold tight, babe."

The world twists, and seconds later Bradley is doubled over, vomiting up whisky, cum, and stomach bile onto the curb of Bay Street.

"Let it out, honey, things are only going to get worse," the ghost says, patting a fuzzy hand on his back.

"How the fuck did we get to Toronto?" Bradley's voice is discordant as he reaches for his holster, forgetting he is wearing nothing but thirty-year-old boxer shorts. "And you still haven't told me who you are."

"We don't have time for logistics, but you can call me Martha. I'm a guide of sorts."

"Where did you come from?" Bradley hesitates, remembering some bullshit email from HR scolding him for asking Mai—*or was it Lai?*—where she was from.

"Neither here nor there. I guess you could say the past, present, and future." Martha shrugs. "Look over there—is it familiar?"

A billboard for *Raiders of the Lost Ark* stands thirty feet tall. Bradley takes in Harrison Ford's angular jaw and half-open shirt, filling in the blanks with his imagination, and a car on the busy twilit street below.

"A Mercury Bobcat," he whispers. "I had one of those."

"Look a little farther."

Tearing his eyes away from nostalgia, Bradley looks beyond the car. Wedged between neon signs and busy clubs with long lines outside is a nondescript brick-fronted building with a brown awning that reads CLUB TORONTO. Before Bradley can say anything, a dozen police cars pull up in front and spill out officers onto the street. Martha touches Bradley's hand again, and suddenly they are inside, at the bottom of a blue-tiled staircase, inhaling the smell of salt and sweat. A memory begins to rush back at Bradley, but it doesn't need to, because in the sudden stream of uniformed officers filing down the stairs, he sees himself. Forty years younger.

Bradley does not remember being so scrawny. He does remember the fear, though. The panic in his young, clear blue eyes exactly reflects how he'd felt that day. More experienced officers brush past him, shouting and raising guns and batons at the naked men in the bath-house. Men who were intertwined moments before spring apart or grab towels to cover themselves. Some, mainly younger ones, remain still in shock, while others walk toward the police, arms outstretched in resignation.

"I ... didn't know what I was doing ... I didn't want to be there," Bradley says, looking up at Martha.

"I never asked for your excuses, Bradley, but thank you for shar-ing," Martha says, dispassionately watching the scene before them like they had seen it a thousand times.

"Why have you brought me here?" Bradley asks, rage rising inside him again. The jarring image of a beefy uniformed officer arresting a naked teenager plays out before him.

Martha answers his question with a question. "Is this why you never came out to your colleagues? Is this why Derick's wife thinks he plays golf on Sundays?"

"I ..." Bradley begins, but Martha's hand is in his again, and they twist into darkness.

With nothing left in his stomach, Bradley dry heaves before assess-ing his surroundings. *Still Toronto*. He spots an Al Gore groupie and a PlayStation 2 advertisement. The same brick-fronted building, a little updated. *Is it 1999, 2000?*

"What's your excuse this time?" Martha asks. Five men—a forty-year-old Bradley among them—try to act casual under the brown awning. Plainclothes officers. Just as quickly as the last time, but with less show, they enter the bathhouse and, minutes later, lead struggling patrons up the stairs and out onto the street, shoving them unceremoni-ously into black Ford Crown Victorias. "Lesbians, really?" Martha says. "What did they do to you?"

"It was unlawful! To ..."

"To what?"

"Gather ... as they did."

"*Gather as they did.*" Martha's tone is mocking. "And where were you last night, Bradley?"

"Things have changed."

"Changed, huh? Then explain this."

Bradley feels Martha become colder and darker beside him, their body radiating with static.

Twisting. Darkness. Nausea.

A group of teenagers in medical masks stand on a street corner, filming a TikTok video. "We're back in the present," Bradley says, stating the obvious. And back in Vancouver.

Through the crowd of people waiting for the 99 bus, Bradley makes out a circle of protestors blocking off the Cambie and Broadway intersection. *Why do they always fucking do that?* he thinks. *Fucking attention seekers.*

Before it happens, Bradley knows what is coming. He watches himself and Derick dismount their 2008 Harley-Davidson Kings and enter the crowd. They walk side by side, careful to keep a few feet between them, careful not to accidentally touch hands. Social distancing before it was cool.

"They were provoking us," he says to Martha, who is now granite grey, almost frozen. Their softness has become dagger-like, the once-sheer glittery halo now sharp, like icicles. They offer no responses.

A man in a red pickup truck is hollering out his window, yelling at the protestors to move. The protestors remain steadfast, chanting things that Bradley does not understand, but knows he hates. One line rings louder than the rest.

"Fuck the police!" Their voices are swelling in unison, vibrating across the hot, dry air.

Some protestors return expletives to the truck driver. He swings open the door, but waits for the automatic step to whir down. It's anticlimactic until he's on the tarmac, and then he's down, turning over and over with a man his same size, but on the opposite end of the melanin spectrum. Present-Bradley and past-Bradley watch the blur of light and dark skin and tarmac.

"The white guy threw the first punch!" a passerby shouts, but it's too late; both Bradleys are running, mirroring each other's movements.

Suddenly, the scene stops, like Netflix when it asks, *Are you still watching?* Martha walks into the middle of the crosswalk, where the now-frozen circle of protestors are watching the commotion. Martha is no longer a shimmering, sweet-scented figure. Their curls are upended, crackling, as if drawing friction from the atmosphere. Their eyes are a deep crimson.

"You're a fucking monster, Bradley, do you know that?"

"Me?" Bradley yells back. "Look at yourself! Who are you to question me, you freak! What are you? A man? A woman? What?"

"Does it matter? I am more human than you will ever be." Martha is circling him now, a cold storm whipping up around them. London Drugs and Whole Foods fade into nothingness.

Bradley blinks and finds himself in a wide, tall-backed wooden chair. Looking down, he sees his wrinkled, calloused hands involuntarily clutching the armrests. Leather straps cut into his wrists, shins, ankles.

"W-what is happening?" Bradley feels numb, his body spent from a heart rate not suited to sexagenarians. A warmth trickles down between his thighs and *drip-drip-drips* on the concrete.

"You know, I've done this a hundred times. And every time, they beg for forgiveness. Tax evaders, serial killers ... but you? You'd rather wear a blue uniform than kiss the man you love in public. And Jayden ... did his life mean nothing to you? Do you feel any guilt at all?"

Martha is just a voice now. But other people are there, some ghostlike figures, some fully formed humans, and others in between. They stare at Bradley through a wide, dirty window. Jayden is in the front row, small again, blinking slowly. Derick is beside him, equally still, and then his wife and their son.

"So?" Martha's voice booms from everywhere and nowhere. "Any remorse?"

"I did my time! Six months administrative leave," Bradley yells and winces as his own voice ricochets back at him like a cold wind. Silence. He breathes into it, his breaths short and anguished.

*A fucking monster.* Martha's words ring in his head. Bradley sees his reflection in the smeared window, his own face superimposed over Jayden's as he sits, blinking, on the front bench. Bradley feels a cool, heavy burning in his chest, and a quiet gasp leaves his mouth. He thinks of the young men, his peers, in the bathhouse, and the kids at the intersection of Cambie and Broadway. He thinks of Derick's wife. *A fucking monster.*

He notices his father in the back row of the bleachers-style seating. He is wearing his 1970s uniform, his navy-blue peaked hat sitting neatly on his head as if he's at a formal event. "Good job, son," his father had said for the first and last time as Bradley descended the wooden stairs, police certificate in hand. "You're a hero now, don't let them tell you otherwise." The memory brings a tingle to Bradley's nose, and his mouth rises upward in a half smile.

*A hero. A fucking hero.*

"I'm a fucking hero," he whispers and looks up, surprised that the words left his mouth, because for the first time, he is unsure if they are true.

Before he can take them back, the window explodes. Fragments of glass burst in slow motion into the room. Bradley watches, waiting for the pain of a thousand cuts. The room dissolves around him, the audience vanishes, and only Bradley remains, still tied to the chair. The glass fragments twist and turn in the air, missiles aiming for their target.

"Wait, I—"Blood catches in Bradley's throat. Hundreds of shards puncture his body. One large piece of glass drives itself through his chest, swift and smooth, like a bullet. He opens his mouth one more time, to call for Martha or Derick or his father, but in his moment of indecision, his final breath catches on the invisible particles passing through him and, like a ghost, it floats into nothing.

# FLORAL ARRANGEMENT I.

## Kai Cheng Thom

I am the venus flytrap femme, the snapback femme, the carniflora
amora devora femme. the femme with open jaw and gaping maw,
drooling perfumed psychotropic saliva. i am that femme of fleshy
petals and hothouse clime, i am a climbing femme with strangling
vines. the clinging femme, the singing femme, the femme who eats
her lovers to stay alive. i am the thriving femme—you call me
conniving femme, but i call myself the girl who gets what she wants.
i am the femme who loves her teeth, and i've got meals to hunt,
so let's keep this brief: i am the femme who stays alive.

# THE CALL
David Ly

**WE KISSED, HENRY THOUGHT TO HIMSELF** as he stumbled out of the elevator to get back to his dorm room. If only the floor would stop undulating like waves beneath his shoes, his trek down the hall would be easier. *He kissed. Me.* Henry smirked, going back to the moment right before Colin's lips had landed on his—how his nerves bubbled in his chest, melted away when they kissed, and finally were drawn out of him when Colin pulled back after playfully biting Henry's bottom lip. Half of Henry's mind giddily relished the memory of the kiss, while the other half reflected that it probably hadn't been a good idea to take edibles before the end-of-semester campus party *and* to drink.

It had seemed like a good idea; he wanted to be at ease, to feel less of the anxiety that crept in his chest at gatherings, and maybe even to be more approachable, rather than his standoffish self (according to his friends). He usually hated going to these things—going out, in general—and preferred to stay cooped up alone in his dorm watching *How to Get Away with Murder* reruns while slurping instant ramen. But tonight's outing needed to happen. It was his final year. He wanted to break out of his mundane routine and let loose, rather than maintain the uptightness that had plagued him for the last year.

After an entire year of walking by the all-glass Aquatics Centre on the way to lit class, nonchalantly peering in at Colin and his swim team during practice, Henry knew they would be at the party thanks to an awkward run-in with Colin last week. Though they were in the same literature class, Henry had never said a word to Colin, let alone had an entire conversation with him. They exchanged friendly nods, but neither ever approached the other. Henry chalked it all up to the fact that he wasn't on the swim team, like all of Colin's other friends. It wasn't until classes were nearly over that Henry had been waiting for his friends outside the Aquatics Centre, so they could meet up for lunch after class, when Colin nearly collided into him.

"Whoops, sorry," Colin stuttered, stopping in his tracks.

Henry froze, then quickly gave a delayed "You too" before feeling his cheeks go warm.

Colin chuckled, flashing his dimples before looking down at the book Henry was holding. "The movie of that wasn't too bad."

"Yeah, it was really good," Henry agreed, though the only thing he'd enjoyed about the *The Great Gatsby* film was Lana Del Rey's contribution to its soundtrack, "Young and Beautiful."

"Never really understood the thing about the green light, but the movie was really cool looking," Colin continued.

"Yeah, I don't get it either." Henry did, in fact, understand the green light, but he wanted more than anything for this conversation to go on indefinitely.

Colin was just about to say something else when one of his swim teammates—unfamiliar to Henry—approached, shouting, "See you at the party tonight?"

"You bet, Tom!" Colin shouted back. "You coming, too?" he asked Henry.

"Uhh ..."

"You should! Might not be as glamorous as a party in the 1920s, but could be fun. We could meet up."

Before Henry could decide what to say, "sure" slipped out of his mouth. For a moment, he felt sure he was going to black out.

"Awesome, see you there," Colin said, giving Henry an awkward pat on the shoulder. For a brief moment, Henry sensed shyness from Colin. A bit of hesitancy. He saw Tom teasingly grab Colin's shoulders, laughing, and Colin shying away, but smiling as they entered the Aquatics Centre.

Henry couldn't believe that had happened only last week. Now he was slamming his body into his dorm room door. He eventually twisted the doorknob and stumbled through. He swiftly removed all of his clothes, then grabbed his water bottle and drained it before falling onto his squeaky single mattress and burritoing himself with the blanket. The last thing he remembered was his drool pooling on the pillow, uncomfortably cold against his chin.

In his dream, Henry was back at the party in the woods. He noticed the fires burned crystal blue and green, the flames moving slower than they should've been. People were running around him, screaming and laughing. He shouted, but no sound left his mouth. Suddenly Colin materialized before his eyes, dripping wet, the way he looked every time he climbed out of the pool. The fire's glow lit his face in a haunting, mesmerizing manner, reflecting off his brown eyes and accentuating the sheen of the damp, black hair that fell in front of his face. He brushed back his hair, and that was when Henry noticed that Colin was wearing only his Speedos, his tight body glistening in the firelight.

Again, the kiss happened. Only this time it was rougher. As Henry tasted Colin's tongue, he could hear Colin's voice in his mind, muttering something undiscernible. They continued kissing. Harder. Colin slipped his tongue in deeper, and the muttering in Henry's head grew louder, though not any clearer. His eyes widened when he felt Colin's tongue slide down his throat. He felt like maybe he should push away, but he allowed Colin to continue ...

Henry shivered as a coldness overcame his body, and he awoke, startled at the dampness around his legs.

He grabbed his phone to check the time, the sudden brightness of the screen making him squint ... 7:42 a.m. He had been asleep only five hours. He grunted and felt for the blanket to kick it off. *Seriously?* He wasn't sure what he was more pissed about: that he had woken from an intensely sexy dream he wished could've gone on longer, or that the dream had woken him with wet sheets. He'd thought wet dreams stopped after puberty. Reaching around in the dark, he felt underneath the blanket and immediately pulled his hand back out when he felt the warm slime on his thighs. *Gross.*

He jumped out of bed to clean up, but crumbled under his own weight, landing with an *oof* as if his legs couldn't support him. Still tangled in the blanket, he tried wiggling his feet, his toes, but the lack of response sent adrenalin surging through his body. Heart pounding, feeling more awake than his five hours' worth of sleep, he grabbed his phone off the nightstand and shone the light down on the blanket while trying to kick himself free.

He couldn't muster the strength to scream. Instead, he just stared in disbelief at the blue-brown tentacles that extended down from his waist. The phone light reflected off the shiny skin slick with slime. The tentacles were entangled together and slowly moving, as if they had a mind of their own. *What the fuck* ... Panic took over, and he threw himself back out from under the blanket, crashing in the dark— he was still trying to stand, but the tentacles wouldn't allow him to. He began sweating, unsure whether to yell for help or not. Eventually, he managed to grab the side of his bed and pull himself up. Resting on his elbows, he was able to reach the lamp on the nightstand. He flicked it on.

Henry stayed like this for a moment, tasting the salty sweat beading down his face and trying to ignore the squishing sound that the—his— tentacles made as they slid over each other and around the ground. He was too afraid to look down. Muttering to himself to stay calm, his eyes fell on the bottle of anxiety meds on his nightstand. Those magical yellow pills. He briefly considered whether it would do any good to take one now, but shrugged it off as a silly idea: the pills wouldn't work fast enough in this moment.

So he found himself resorting to an exercise his counsellor had taught him. In the dim lamplight, Henry looked around the room and tried to count three items of every colour. The blue cover of an English literature anthology, the translucent-blue pill bottle, and the blue stripe on a rainbow pin that sat on his desk—he'd never bothered to pin it to his backpack. Next was black, and it was easier to find three black items, but when it came to yellow, he was stumped. His pills only counted as one item, and nothing else in his room was yellow. He reached over and tapped his phone to see that fifteen minutes had passed.

"Shit," he whispered, then fell into deep breaths, abandoning the coloured-items exercise. As he breathed, he felt his tentacles writhing on the ground, moving overtop the fibres of the cheap carpet; the tentacles snagged, but he could feel the suckers pushing away. One of his tentacles wandered farther from the rest, straying off to the side and looping itself through his backpack on the ground. Without a single thought from him, it managed to slowly unzip the bag's front pocket. Henry could imagine seeing what the tentacle saw as it moved into the pocket, probing in the dark.

And then suddenly, he tasted it: a dried blueberry muffin. The more the tentacle wrapped itself around the muffin, the more Henry could taste it, but not in his mouth—with the suckers of the tentacle. Exploring more, his mouth fell slightly ajar. He swallowed saliva pooling on his tongue—a reflex every time the tentacle landed on an extra sweet spot of muffin.

"Henry?" a voice shouted, followed by banging on his door. The tentacle quickly withdrew from the backpack. Not realizing it until it had already happened, Henry was miraculously standing on two legs again, legs that were bare and slick with slime. The ground was slightly spongy with slime, as well. "Henry, are you awake?" the voice called. Henry looked around for his underwear, slipped it on, and tried to wipe off as much of the slime from his legs as possible before walking over to the door and opening it a bit.

"Hi?" Henry croaked. At first, Henry didn't recognize the face at his door. A few seconds later, he recalled that it was Tom, one of Colin's friends who'd been at the party. Henry vaguely recalled that at some point during his buzz, he'd been hovering at the keg, chatting with Colin and Tom, and had said something that made them both laugh. He wished he could remember what. Henry cleared his throat and said "hi" again.

Tom looked him up and down. "Did it happen? Put some clothes on. Let's go!" Before Henry could answer, Tom backed from the door and turned to walk away. "Colin wants to see you. He was too nervous to come get you this morning, so he sent me," he said over his shoulder, half smiling.

Colin? Nervous? "Wait!" Henry almost swung the door wide open, but realized he needed to get dressed first. He shut the door and quickly put on a pair of black sweat shorts and a dark-blue tank top that smelled clean enough, then slipped into his runners. Out in the hallway, he caught up to Tom. "What do you mean, 'Did it happen'?"

Tom stopped and turned, looking Henry up and down again. "It's always weird when they first come. It feels like you don't have any control over them, doesn't it?" Henry stared blankly back at Tom. "Don't worry. It gets better. Not completely, but you'll learn to trust them to lead you, instead of worrying if you're going in the right direction."

Henry felt like he should've been more confused, but something about what Tom was saying made him feel understood. He took a deep breath.

"Where are we going?"

Tom was already heading down the stairs. "Let's go, c'mon." Henry ran down after him, trying to keep up.

It was an early spring morning, bright, but still chilly. Henry wished he had put on more layers. He followed Tom as they headed down the road to the side of campus where the stairs down to the beach were, the stairs that always left Henry's legs sore whenever his friends dragged him down to the beach for a hangout, forgetting they'd have to walk back up drunk. As Tom descended the steps, leaping down them, Henry struggled to even walk down the steep incline.

"Could you tell me what this is all about?"

"We had a good time with you at the party! Colin wants to see you again. Was too shy to come get you himself, I told you already." Tom's voice echoed back up as he descended from Henry's vision. *Goddamn athletes ...* What exactly did *we had a good time with you* mean? Henry couldn't remember much, and he was worried about what Tom meant by it. He was two-thirds of the way down the stairs now, and the cool air clung to his still-slimy legs, which made him even colder. It was pretty uncomfortable running down the steps like this—running at all, for Henry—let alone this early in the morning. Finally, he made it to the bottom and heaved over, hands on his knees, trying to breathe, but not too deeply, as the cold air coming in from the ocean hurt his throat every time he inhaled. *Goddamn athletes ...*

Looking up, he could see Tom chatting with some other swimmers whose names Henry knew in passing from his literature class: Kenji, Markus, and Quin ... and Colin. The first three were laughing at something Tom had said, but Colin stepped away from the group, threw Henry a smile, and waved him over. Colin was shirtless, barefoot, and in his underwear. *Okay, so this is happening.*

Standing up straight and taking in a deep breath, Henry strolled over, trying to act nonchalant while kicking up sand with every step. He hoped it wasn't apparent that he was still trying to catch his breath.

"It's good to see you again," Colin said, walking over to meet Henry halfway. The rest of the guys nodded over at him.

"Yeah ... what's going on?"

"How's the hangover? Weird dreams?" Colin smirked.

"Uhh ..."

Colin laughed, which made Henry feel awkward, so he tried to join in on the joke, chuckling.

"We're about to go swim, and I wanted you to come with."

"Oh, uh, I don't swim. In the ocean? Now? It's freezing, isn't it? I don't swim. Not like you guys. Well, I don't really swim at all, actually." He caught himself rambling and stopped. The sound of the waves crashing onto the shore filled the awkward silence. He looked past Colin's shoulder, at the others. They were stripping off, throwing their clothes in a pile. They ran naked into the water, shouting at each other, making jokes, laughing. They waded out, eventually diving under. Henry shivered at the thought of jumping into the water.

"You okay?"

"It's just so cold," Henry half laughed.

"Yeah, it's kind of refreshing though, isn't it?" Colin began walking over to the water, motioning Henry to follow. Without much thought, Henry slipped out of his shoes and followed. They stood with their feet in the dark sand as the icy water splashed against them.

"I've been wanting to talk to you for a while. I always saw you walking by the Aquatics Centre. I'm glad we were able to hang out at that party."

Henry kept wondering what they were doing out here. It was completely out of character for him to do something so impulsive like this.

"I, uh, don't usually go out to those things. Sorry if last night was ..." He was rambling again.

"I'm glad you came. Sorry if I was awkward last week," Colin flashed a smile. "Wanna swim?"

They held each other's gaze. Worried it might be too long, Henry glanced out at the ocean and realized he hadn't seen Marcus, Kenji, Quin, or Tom ever since they'd gone in. "Where'd they go?"

"C'mon." Colin grabbed Henry's hand and ran into the water.

"It's cold!" Henry screamed for Colin to stop, but he was also enjoying all of it.

They were up to their waists now. Colin turned and kissed Henry slowly. As he did, Henry heard it again: that chanting, or was it singing now? Colin's voice in his head whispering unfamiliar words. The adrenalin and panic that charged through Henry's body eventually subsided when Colin pulled away.

"Ready?"

"I don't know," Henry said, shivering. He couldn't feel his legs anymore.

Colin grabbed Henry's wrist tighter and, without warning, dove into the water, pulling Henry down with him. The shock of cold water on his chest almost knocked the breath out of Henry, but he held it as Colin pulled him farther out into the ocean. Farther and farther, they swam side by side now, still holding hands. Henry felt like he couldn't hold his breath for much longer and yanked for Colin to stop—he did. Underwater, Henry watched as Colin patted his own chest, opened his mouth, inhaled the water, then exhaled bubbles through his nose. He put a hand on Henry's chest, who shook his head in a panic, but Colin grabbed both of Henry's hands as they remained suspended in the water.

Colin kept on breathing underwater, and when the breath-holding became unbearable for Henry, he fell into Colin's rhythm and took his first inhale. As the water went into his lungs, the sensation was like ice crystalizing the blood in his veins, but the coolness spread throughout his entire body, waking him, calming him. He took deeper breaths, marvelling at it all. Breathing now with his eyes closed, Henry felt his body relax, his muscles untense.

When he opened his eyes again, he saw that Colin had transformed. His reddish-brown tentacles swirled about him, and his underwear drifted down. Henry watched in amazement, inspecting each of Colin's tentacles, until he gazed down at himself and realized that his own tentacles had appeared, his shorts now drifting down to follow Colin's underwear. Henry felt silly with his tank top still on, so he slipped out of that as well. Unlike when he'd first seen them in his room, his tentacles were much livelier. He could feel them treading water so that he wouldn't sink. Every now and then he could taste the saltiness of the water through them. He smiled at Colin, his tentacles beginning to drift out toward him. Henry tried to stop them, but they were moving with a mind of their own, like when one of them had ventured into his backpack to taste the blueberry muffin.

At first, Henry's tentacles retracted as soon as their tips briefly touched Colin's. A moment later, they reached out again. Their tentacles intertwined. Henry was being pulled toward Colin. As their faces slowly drifted closer together, Henry could feel Colin's heartbeat through his tentacles. He focused on Colin's rhythmic calmness, while he felt his own heartbeat quickening. The faster his heart went, the tighter Colin's tentacles gripped him. Colin explored Henry's body, tasting his skin through each of his suckers. Henry closed his eyes, feeling Colin's tentacles kiss him all over. Each time their tentacles touched, he could taste Colin: sweetness mixed into the salty seawater. His skin goosebumped as Colin explored further. The back of his neck. His lower ribs. The portion where his torso flowed into his tentacles was surprisingly sensitive.

*Are you doing okay?*

It was Colin's voice in his head. Henry whipped his head up and opened his eyes wide to look at Colin.

*How?*

Colin smiled, flashing teeth. Henry hadn't noticed before, but Colin's teeth were all much sharper now. Like little pearly daggers. And his eyes—his eyes were a ghostly white. *We've finally met.* Colin looked down at his tentacles spinning around Henry's. *That's how you can understand me now.*

*But what's happening? Did you ... do this to me?* Henry asked, waving two tentacles around under his own control now.

*No, not exactly. From what I've been told, we've always had them. It seems like it takes something out of the ordinary for the tentacles to show themselves. Right place, right time.* Colin swam around Henry before stopping in front of him again, holding his hands, their faces close. *The right person.* Henry wondered if his own teeth and eyes had changed as well. *I know how it feels sometimes. The nerves. Being in the water helped me with that.*

Colin was right. Henry felt lighter here. With Colin. Two boys suspended in the water.

As if out of nowhere, Kenji, Markus, Quin, and Tom came bursting through the darkness below, their tentacles propelling them. They darted left and right, gliding up and plunging down before coming back up and swimming around Henry and Colin. Henry could feel the currents of their movements against his body as they playfully swam about.

Colin let go of his hands, and Henry drifted backwards, his tentacles reaching out for Colin's as they drifted farther apart. He was right. There was a calmness to everything. As the four others zipped around, Henry closed his eyes and allowed their currents to push and pull him any which way. He didn't want to resist. He didn't feel the *need* to resist. His body told him it was okay to just do nothing in the moment. He could hear the boys, but not in his head, like Colin. They whistled and clicked, chattering to each other, it seemed, creating a music that put him even more at ease.

When he opened his eyes, he found that he was lying horizontally in the water, looking down into the dark depths below. He could feel the thick, inky darkness staring back. There was something *alive* about it, and though it made him nervous, he still stared. At the sides of his vision, Kenji, Markus, Quin, and Tom began swimming calmly down into it.

Colin grabbed Henry's hands, positioning him upright again.

*What's down there?* Henry asked.

*Something that helped us.*

Uncertainty crept into Henry's body. But looking into the darkness, he felt curious about it. Instead of fighting it, he let the anxiety fill him. This time, though, he wasn't drowning in it.

*Do we go down there?* Henry asked.

*Only if you want.*

Henry watched the tips of the other boys' tentacles disappear into the dark.

*I do, a little.*

Colin held Henry's hand. *We can go together, then.*

# HIDEOUS CREATURES

## Jane Shi

*after Cyrée Jarelle Johnson*

what is a monster made of but brittle skin
and light projections about violence? Victor
forgot to bathe, dim, turn off, cool, soothe
sensory gash / each rehash—until we hear
thoughts again. you bring in guns to tame
us, and before that, words: "aggressive,"
"violent," "unsafe." soft power post-Tumblr
pop psychology experiments on correctable.

what is a monster made of but bodies?
in another telling, the creature found
a companion in a competitor's lab, made
to blink think read everything instant
gratification but whose gratification
did you really create then eat the meat
of savants just to envy us? you Entrapta
us in a wire web. you electroshock us

a monster map of nerve, nerve, pain.
what did you expect, victor of history?
you wonder if we are monsters but never
heard—*monere*—our porous warnings:
two autists in love can rebuild the world.
a foretaste of those icy climes made you
want to destroy us. at the end of our
letters we survive. at the end we survive.

what is a monster but extracts of shame.
soft vanilla perfume perfectible chisels
of seamless systems you call community.
can we rebuild this world with you? after
our hands ruined your cake sheets you
abandoned us. you abandoned us. but
even the most hideous creatures deserve
a chance to wail, fail, and then try again.

# LIKE ME

Daniel Zomparelli

**I HAVEN'T LEFT MY APARTMENT IN THREE DAYS.** It's so fucking annoying, like I want to go and do something but I am just stuck here. I just keep thinking about being outside four days ago, wandering the mall below my apartment and trying to find new photo moments, but honestly I've already tapped this mall dry. I've lived here for six months, and you'd think they'd have a new store or new product for me to promote to add to my brand, but I am just so fucking over it. And I'm like, so fucking depressed. I saw all of my friends, or like I guess they were my friends, over at Fire Island doing their end-of-summer posts. They did like a whole group shot where everyone is laughing and having the best time and I'm just like, so broke so I'm stuck here. Fuck.

So anyway, you're like oh my god Brandon, why are you stuck in your apartment and I am all blah blah blah blah blah. Okay well, I'm such a stupid shit, I like, ran out of space on my credit card because like, I'm still waiting on all of these ads to pay out and those rumours of me buying followers is not true! I talked to one guy about wishing for more followers but that's not the same, and so I'm starving or whatever, and I tweet it out and one of my followers is all, "I can help!" and so I let him. He gets here, and he's like, obsessed with me, like sad obsessed, it's gross but also kind of hot. So he just comes here and says he'll help and I'm all, buy me a pizza, and get this: he has no money. Nothing. He comes here broke, trying to help.

So he's all, I can make something, and he heads to my kitchen and I only have seltzer water and an old bottle of melon liqueur so I'm thinking he's going to make me a seltzer fucking melon sushi or whatever, and he comes back with his hand on a plate. Like, just his severed hand on a plate, and like, I'm not eating that! I scream at him to clean the blood up from my carpet because this is a rental and I'm not eating a raw hand, so he goes back to the kitchen and I hear the microwave going so now I have to see what this idiot is doing, and he's holding a kitchen towel to his stump of an arm and his hand is turning circles in the microwave. And like, he pulls out Taco Bell hot sauce from his bag, swag LOL oh my god Beyoncé moment, and he hands me back the plate with a smattering of taco sauce. It looks so disgusting, but I'm not a monster so I try it but it's so gross I just lick the sauce and he's so disappointed, but he tells me he'll get another one of my followers to help him.

So this other guy comes up and he's just standing there confused because I guess he also has no money, and I am not kidding he straight up snaps his own neck because he's embarrassed, so now I'm like, stuck with this fucking dead guy at my doorway and like this is my version of a Fire Island vacation, just a bunch of useless followers falling apart around me. And another thing about Fire Island, like I was a part of that crew for so long, and then all of a sudden they jump up in followers from like 30 thousand which is fucking respectable, to like 800 thousand which sounds like a scam, and they just don't invite me anymore. Like, I was the first one to do this, and I created the hashtag #fireguysland so like, I should sue them or something, but I am above it, obviously, with everything now. But I just think it's funny.

So anyway, this dead guy, we try and move him to the couch and it's like *Weekend at Bernie's*, except he's so fucking heavy that we need another person to help so I ask another follower and like, seven show up, it's so embarrassing like I just need one person I don't need like a whole fucking pit crew, I'm not RuPaul, you guys are literally the best and so supportive of me. So they move him and they are all asking me what else I need, but I'm so tired and I ask them to just let me nap or whatever and I joke about being so disappointed, but just a joke because like, that's my humour and if you don't get it or you're offended, unfollow, but they all just snap their necks just like in the movies. So I have all these bodies here and their necks are so weird and mangled and some are blocking the doorway, and how am I supposed to even get out? Some people take me so seriously. So I ask the one-handed guy to help me move them from the door, but that idiot bled out.

And, okay, I know I keep bringing this up, but not even asking me to go to Fire Island is so rude. I get it, you were all like more of an influencer than me, but did I invite other people below me whenever I went, always. Who else takes the photos? I mean, I can take a photo. It's just so rude, it makes me so mad. Whatever, I'm so over it.

Anyway. So this time maybe it was my fault because I got more followers to come over to move the others, but when they got inside the apartment I thought it would be fun if we did a human pyramid for a photoshoot and it just did not work, they kept stumbling and I am so stupid and yelled out that we should all just kill ourselves because it was so bad but it was a joke but they all rushed to the kitchen, grabbed my dull-ass kitchen knives, and immediately killed themselves. And like, I love to be heard, like really heard so I appreciated them so much in that moment, because sometimes I feel like no one listens to me and to be truly heard is such a gift.

But after that there were so many bodies that I couldn't move them, and I was so tired and dehydrated that I just lay back on all these bodies, but the lighting was kind of perfect, and I just did a quick snap.

And it was so good. I mean, you all saw. Like, obviously so many of you are new followers, hi guys, check out my fan account, link in bio where you can get merch, which will ship out as soon as I can get out of here I promise.

So anyway, here I am just watching my followers grow. I can't believe I'm finally getting the followers I deserve. Like, #fireguysland follower numbers. I just didn't expect it to come like this, trapped in my apartment. And like, I did wish for this. I met this one guy who was like so creepy, but kind of sexy, and he was like make a wish, and it was this. And it was weird when he asked for my soul or whatever, but honestly I already gave up my soul to my SoulCycle instructor ha ha am I right? But yeah this guy was like weird and kept calling himself the puzzle master or something. Honestly I wasn't really listening, I was just thinking about my followers.

Wait, hold on. Okay it looks like they're not dead! Okay, they are getting up. Great, ugh, I can finally get out of my apartment. And like, so many of you are here now supporting me, and I love that. It's exactly what creepy puzzle guy said would happen! And I just appreciate you all showing up, I really do. Ugh, their necks look so weird, but I can totally fix that. You all know I worked for a week in a makeup department and a stick and some strong cover-up will fix it.

I can't believe how blessed I am! So many people just talk about it but you are all here, and so many more are coming, and obviously I would appreciate any more. I can see you all from the window all lined up around the premises. And I know that the police outside are armed, but we are so much bigger than that. Like, I didn't mean to start a war, ha ha, OMG Miley #wreckingball moment! But like, we should finish this. This is my mall now. Okay peace out, so much love to you all, and don't forget to hit that Like button and share!

# CONTRIBUTOR BIOGRAPHIES

**Cicely Belle Blain** is a Black / mixed queer femme of Gambian (Wolof), Jamaican, and English ancestry from London, UK, based on the lands of the Musqueam, Squamish, and Tsleil-Waututh people. They are notable for founding Black Lives Matter Vancouver, as well as being listed as one of *Vancouver Magazine*'s Power 50 in 2018 and 2020 and as one of *Refinery29 Canada*'s 29 Powerhouses. Cicely teaches Executive Leadership at SFU and is the Editorial Director of *Ripple of Change Magazine*. Cicely's debut book of poetry, *Burning Sugar* (Arsenal Pulp Press, 2020), won the 2021 Pat Lowther Memorial Award and was longlisted for the Gerald Lampert Memorial Award.

**Eddy Boudel Tan** is the author of two novels: *After Elias*, a finalist for the ReLit Awards and the Edmund White Award, and *The Rebellious Tide*, a finalist for the Ferro-Grumley Award. In 2021, he was named a Rising Star by the Writers' Trust of Canada. His work depicts a world much like our own—the heroes are flawed, truth is distorted, and there's beauty in the imperfection. His short stories can be found in *Joyland, Yolk, Gertrude Press*, and *The G&LR*. He lives in Vancouver with his husband.
WEB: *eddyboudeltan.com*
TWITTER: *@eddyautomatic*

**Levi Cain** was born in California, raised in Connecticut, and currently lives in Massachusetts. Their first chapbook, *dogteeth.*, was released by Ursus Americanus Press in 2020.
WEB: *levicain.wordpress.com*
INSTAGRAM: *@honestlyliketbh*
TWITTER: *@honestlyliketbh*

**Jessica Cho** is a Rhysling Award–winning writer of short fiction and poetry. Born in Korea, they currently live in New England, where they balance their aversion to cold with the inability to live anywhere without snow. Previous works can be found in *Fireside Fiction*, *Apparition Lit*, *khōreō*, *Flash Fiction Online*, *Anathema*, and others.
WEB: *semiwellversed.wordpress.com*
TWITTER: *@wordsbycho*

**Steven Cordova**'s full-length collection of poetry, *Long Distance*, was published by Bilingual Review Press in 2010. His poems are forthcoming in *Pleiades* and *Hunger Mountain Review* and have appeared in *Bellevue Literary Review*, *The Journal*, *New Orleans Review*, *Notre Dame Review*, and the *Los Angeles Review*. From San Antonio, TX, he lives in Brooklyn, NY.
INSTAGRAM: *@stevengcordova*

**Kayla Czaga** is a teacher, restaurant manager, and the author of two collections of poetry: *For Your Safety Please Hold On* (Nightwood Editions, 2014) and *Dunk Tank* (House of Anansi, 2019). She lives in Victoria, BC.
INSTAGRAM: *@czagazaga*
TWITTER: *@kaylaczaga*

**Amber Dawn** is the editor of the queer weird anthology *Fist of the Spider Woman: Tales of Fear and Queer Desire* (2009). Her debut novel, *Sub Rosa* (2010), is an award-winning sex worker portal dark fantasy, and her sophomore novel, *Sodom Road Exit* (2018), is a mix of paranormal horror and chosen family domestic drama. She teaches speculative fiction writing and other creative genres at Douglas College.

**David Demchuk**'s debut, *The Bone Mother*, won the 2018 Sunburst Award for adult fiction, was nominated for the Scotiabank Giller Prize and the Shirley Jackson Award, and became an Amazon number-one bestseller. His troubling new queer horror novel / memoir, RED X, was published in August by Strange Light, an imprint of Penguin Random House. David was born and raised in Winnipeg before making his home in Toronto.

**Emrys Donaldson** is an Assistant Professor of English at Jacksonville State University whose work has appeared in *Electric Literature*, *TriQuarterly*, DIAGRAM, *The Rumpus*, and other publications.
WEB: *emrysdonaldson.com*
INSTAGRAM: *@emrysdonaldson*
TWITTER: *@emrysdo*

**Justin Ducharme** is a filmmaker and writer from the Métis community of St. Ambroise on Treaty 1 Territory. He is the co-editor of *Hustling Verse: An Anthology of Sex Workers' Poetry*. Justin's writing has been featured in *Canadian Art*, *Sex Worker Wisdom*, *Room Magazine*, and *PRISM International*. He currently lives and works on the unceded Coast Salish territory of the Musqueam, Squamish, and Tsleil-Waututh Nations.
INSTAGRAM: *@jayuhstin*
TWITTER: *@jstindchrme*

**Ryan Dzelzkalns** has poems appearing with *Assaracus*, DIAGRAM, *The Offing*, *The Shanghai Literary Review*, *Tin House*, and others. He received an MFA from New York University and a BA from Macalester College, where he was awarded the Wendy Parrish Poetry Prize. His writing has been translated into Latvian (the language of his grandparents) and has been anthologized in a handful of collections. He was recently a Fulbright scholar in Tokyo, where he still lives.
WEB: *RyanDz.com*
INSTAGRAM: *@ryandzryandz*
TWITTER: *@RyanDzPoet*

**Hiromi Goto** is an emigrant from Japan who gratefully resides in Lekwungen Territory. She's published numerous novels for both adults and youth, as well as a collection of short stories with Arsenal Pulp Press. Her first graphic novel, *Shadow Life*, was published in 2021 with First Second Books.

**Tin Lorica** is a comedian and poet. They have a poetry chapbook with Rahila's Ghost Press called *soft armour*. Tin co-hosts two live shows in Vancouver—one called Millennial Line, a comedy and poetry series, and Yellow Fever: An All-Asian Comedy Show, which has been featured at Just for Laughs Vancouver.

INSTAGRAM: *@selfiemixtape*

TWITTER: *@selfiemixtape*

**Avra Margariti** is a queer author, Greek sea monster, and Pushcart Prize–nominated poet with a fondness for the dark and the darling. Avra's work haunts publications such as *Vastarien, Asimov's, Liminality, Arsenika, The Future Fire, Space and Time, Eye to the Telescope,* and *Glittership. The Saint of Witches*, Avra's debut collection of horror poetry, is forthcoming from Weasel Press.

TWITTER: *@avramargariti*

**Victoria Mbabazi**'s work can be found in several literary magazines, including *Rejection Letters, Minola Review,* and *No Contact Mag.* They're the author of the chapbooks *chapbook* (Anstruther Press) and *FLIP* (KFB press). They live in Brooklyn, New York.

**Saskia Nislow** is a writer, ceramicist, and monster enthusiast currently based in Kansas City, MO.

WEB: *siramuks.com*

INSTAGRAM: *@dirtbagsappho*

TWITTER: *@Dot_Boring*

**Kelly Rose Pflug-Back**'s fiction, poetry, and journalism have appeared in places like the *Toronto Star, Ideomancer Speculative Fiction, Briarpatch, Goblin Fruit, Strange Horizons,* and many others, as well as having won awards from the P.K. Page Irwin Foundation and the Great Canadian Literary Hunt. Her first full-length book of poems, *The Hammer of Witches*, was published with Caitlin Press / Dagger Editions in 2020. She lives on unceded Anishinaabek and Haudenosaunee territories.
INSTAGRAM: *@kellyrosecreates*
TWITTER: *@kellypflug*

**Anton Pooles** was born in Novosibirsk, Siberia, and now lives and writes in Toronto, Ontario, where he edits the poetry journal *Cypress*. His work has appeared in an array of journals and magazines such as *This Magazine, Icefloe Press*, and *Long Con Magazine*. He is the author of the chapbook *Monster 36* (Anstruther Press, 2018) and the full-length collection *Ghost Walk* (Mansfield Press, 2022).

**Ben Rawluk** is a queer writer of fiction and poetry living on the traditional, ancestral, and unceded territories of the šxʷməθkʷəy̓əma?ɬ təməxʷ (Musqueam), Sḵwx̱wú7mesh-ulh Temíx̱w (Squamish), and səl̓ilwəta?ɬ təməxʷ (Tsleil-Waututh). A graduate of the University of British Columbia's Creative Writing MFA program, his work has appeared in *Maisonneuve, Plenitude*, and *Cosmonauts Avenue*, among others.
INSTAGRAM: *@benrawlu*
TWITTER: *@brawluk*

**Jane Shi** is a queer Chinese settler living on the unceded, traditional, and ancestral territories of the Musqueam, Squamish, and Tsleil-Waututh First Nations. Her debut chapbook is *Leaving Chang'e on Read* (Rahila's Ghost Press, 2022). She wants to live in a world where love is not a limited resource, land is not mined, hearts are not filched, and bodies are not violated.

INSTAGRAM: *@pipagaopoetry*

TWITTER: *@pipagaopoetry*

**jaye simpson** (they/them) is an Oji-Cree Saulteaux Indigiqueer from the Sapotaweyak Cree Nation. simpson is a writer, advocate, and activist sharing their knowledge and lived experiences in hope of creating utopia. Their first poetry collection, *it was never going to be okay* (Nightwood), was shortlisted for the 2021 ReLit Award and was a 2021 Dayne Ogilvie Prize finalist, also winning the 2021 Indigenous Voices Award for Published Poetry in English. They are a displaced Indigenous person resisting, ruminating, and residing on xʷməθkʷəy̓əm (Musqueam), səl̓ilwətaʔɬ (Tsleil-Waututh), and sḵwx̱wú7mesh (Squamish) First Nations territories, colonially known as Vancouver.

**Matthew Stepanic** is a queer writer who lives and works on Treaty 6 territory in Edmonton. He is the co-founder of Edmonton's newest bookstore, Glass Bookshop. He is a co-author of the collaborative novel, *Project Compass* (Monto Books, 2017), and the author of *Relying on That Body* (Glass Buffalo Publishing, 2018), a poetry chapbook about *RuPaul's Drag Race*. His work has appeared or is forthcoming in *Poetry Is Dead*, *CV2*, *Eighteen Bridges*, and others.

INSTAGRAM: *@mlstepanic*

**Kai Cheng Thom** is a writer, performer, queer healer, and mediator based in Toronto/tkaronto. She is the author of five award-winning books in multiple genres, including the novel *Fierce Femmes and Notorious Liars: A Dangerous Trans Girl's Confabulous Memoir* and the essay collection *I Hope We Choose Love*. Kai Cheng is a winner of the Dayne Ogilvie Prize and the Publishing Triangle Award, among others. She also writes the advice column Ask Kai: Advice for the Apocalypse.

**Matthew J. Trafford** was once a student at an all-boys Catholic high school, where he furtively read the Anne Rice vampire novels before homeroom and never dreamed that he would one day contribute to an anthology of queer monsters. Happily, it all makes sense now. His collection of stories, *The Divinity Gene*, garnered critical acclaim in Canada and the US. "In Our Own Image" is from his next collection, *Daddy, Diva, Donor, Dude*, which he is working on concurrently with his novel about stillbirth and interdimensional travel. He also writes for the screen and designs knitwear as Fairy Godfather Knits.

**Anuja Varghese** is a Pushcart Prize–nominated writer based in Hamilton, ON. Her work appears in *Hobart*, *The Fiddlehead*, *The Malahat Review*, *Plenitude Magazine*, THIS *Magazine*, and others. She recently completed a collection of short stories and is at work on a debut novel while pursuing a Creative Writing Certificate from the University of Toronto. Anuja is also a professional grant writer and editor, and in 2021, took on the role of Fiction Editor with *The Puritan* magazine.
WEB: *anujavarghese.com*
INSTAGRAM: *@anuja_v*
TWITTER: *@Anuja_V*

**Andrew Wilmot** is an award-winning writer and editor, co-publisher of the magazine *Anathema: Spec from the Margins* (anathemamag .com), and an associate editor for Poplar Press. Their first novel, *The Death Scene Artist*, an epistolary horror story of body dysmorphia, gender dysphoria, and self-destruction, is available from Buckrider Books / Wolsak & Wynn. They are represented by Kelvin Kong of K2 Literary (k2literary.com).

**beni xiao** is a virgo, artist, and author of *Bad Egg* (Rahila's Ghost Press, 2017). They live on the traditional and unceded territories of the Tsleil-Waututh, Musqueam, and Squamish First Nations people.

INSTAGRAM: *@verysmallbear*

TWITTER: *@verysmallbear*

# EDITOR BIOGRAPHIES

Photo credit: Joy-Gyamfi

**David Ly** is a writer, editor, and poet. He is the author of the poetry collections *Mythical Man* (shortlisted for the 2021 ReLit Poetry Award) and *Dream of Me as Water*, both published under Anstruther Books at Palimpsest Press. His poems have appeared in PRISM *international*, *The Puritan*, *Arc Poetry Magazine*, *carte blanche*, *Best Canadian Poetry 2021*, and elsewhere. In 2021, he won the *The Puritan*'s inaugural Austin Clarke Prize in Literary Excellence for Poetry. He currently lives on unceded Coast Salish territory.

Photo credit: Victoria Black

**Daniel Zomparelli** is the author of the poetry collections *Davie Street Translations* and *Rom Com*, co-written with Dina Del Bucchia. His collection of short stories, *Everything Is Awful and You're a Terrible Person*, was nominated for the Ethel Wilson Fiction Prize and won the ReLit Short Fiction Award. It has been translated into three other languages. His podcast, *I'm Afraid That*, was listed as one of the best podcasts of 2018 by *Esquire*. He currently lives in Los Angeles.